THE PRUNE PIT MURDER

A BARKSIDE OF THE MOON COZY MYSTERY
BOOK FIVE

RENEE GEORGE

BARKSIDE OF THE MOON PRESS

Werecougar Lily Mason has sworn off investigating crimes in Moonrise, Missouri. Now that she's a college student with two jobs and officially the girlfriend of animal activist Parker Knowles, she's too busy for drama and danger.

Besides, the last case nearly cost her everything, including her life.

At least until her friend, the elderly Opal Dixon, breaks a hip and must recuperate in a nursing home. Opal has been spending all her time complaining about her annoying roommate, her idiot doctor, and the laundry service that keeps losing her clothes. So, Lily is less than convinced when Opal insists a nurse's suicide is really foul play.

Still, to ease her friend's fears, Lily agrees to look into the situation. With her loyal dog Smooshie at her side while she delves into the case, Lily soon learns that it's not all Bingo and low-sodium diets at Moonrise Manor.

And when Opal's suspicions make her the next target, Lily realizes she's running out of time to save her friend...and stop a desperate killer.

ACKNOWLEDGMENTS

First, I have to thank **Lauren Allen** of the **Missouri Pit Bull Rescue** organization for patiently answering each one of my questions about pit bull rescue (no matter how crazy they might have been). Thank you for sharing the stories of success and failure you all experience in your quest to save this wonderful breed. I encourage everyone who loves dogs to donate to this group (www.mopitbullrescue.org) as they build their new shelter that will allow them to house even more rescues until they can be placed in foster or forever homes. The shelter in my book is more well-funded than real life shelters, but that is the benefit of fiction. There is not nearly enough money, volunteers, or space at most of these places to help all the pit bulls who need to be rescued. Any mistakes I may have written about "pit bull rescue" are mine and mine alone.

Second, I have to thank my BFF sister Robbin Clubb. This book happened in large part to your patience, careful reads, mega encouragement, and great suggestions. I love you to the moon!

To the fans of Lily and Smooshie, I will keep writing these stories as long as you want to keep reading them. These are love letters to my obsession with whodunits and my obsession with my pit bull Kona. Thank you for taking this ride with me! <3

Last, I want to thank coffee for keeping me going. Thank you, Coffee. Thank you, thank you.

For My Mother-In-Law Ruby.

CHAPTER 1

A blond man in his forties, wearing a white dress shirt and tan pants, slapped his hand onto the nurses' station counter at Moonrise Manor, one of three nursing homes in Moonrise, Missouri.

"I don't give a tinker's damn what the daughter-in-law wants," he said. "Mrs. Davidson doesn't need a complete blood chemistry and tox screen. The tests aren't going to tell me anything I don't already know. The reason her blood glucose was high is that she's type one diabetic. The reason she's confused is because she's terminally old."

The red-faced young blonde behind the desk replied, "Yes, Dr. Smith." She wore peach scrubs with the name Abby R. LPN on a name tag, along with a pinched expression of disapproval. "I'll pass that message on to her family."

"Don't be so impertinent, Abby," Dr. Smith huffed. He immediately tempered his tone. "Just tell Jenna Davidson that I've ordered the blood test." He stormed off down the hall the way we'd—meaning Hannah Batterman and I—had come in with Paula Jackson, the nursing home's social worker. Paula looked like she was trying hard to pretend the interaction between the nurse and the doctor hadn't taken place in a public area.

"That's awkward," Hannah whispered to me. "I know Jenna Davidson. I'm not sure that doctor wants to tangle with her. She's a hellcat."

Paula interrupted whatever else Hannah was going to say. "We're so happy to have Smiley come visit with the residents."

The white pit bull terrier, wearing a blue vest with a Therapy Dog patch on one side and a "Please Pet Me" patch on the other, perked up at hearing his name.

Paula reached down and tentatively patted the dog's head. "The activity room is just down the hall here on the left."

I'd agreed to come down with Hannah since it was my last Friday before fall classes started, and I had the afternoon off from both Petry's Pet Clinic and the Moonrise Pit Bull Rescue. I couldn't believe I was finally going to start my last two semesters of the Veterinarian Technician program at Two Hills Community College. Honestly, until I had moved to Moonrise, I never believed things like second chances and fresh starts were possible. Paradise Falls, where I'd grown up, had felt like a prison. Moonrise had been my freedom walk.

My girl Smooshie, a large rusty-red and white pit bull, was hanging out with Grandpa Greer for the afternoon, which freed me up to observe Hannah and Smiley's therapy session.

An older woman, slightly overweight, wearing a blue skirt, colorful peasant blouse, and sensible shoes, stood in an open door. I noticed a mild tremor in her hands as she waved at us.

Hannah smiled. "That's Annie Blankenship, the activity director," she told me. "She arranged today for Smiley and me."

Smiley wagged his tail, and he pranced down the hall with us, his claws clicking across the tile as we made our way to Annie.

Smiley, an affectionate and gentle boy from our rescue, had recently completed a stringent obedient course, including the American Kennel Club's Good Citizen, Distraction Proof, and Therapy Dog training. His forever mom, Hannah, had taken him to comfort patients on the children's ward at the hospital twice, and now, to bring joy to seniors at the nursing home. Seven more therapy visits would earn Smiley an AKC Therapy Novice certification.

Hannah, a high school drama teacher and single mom, had fallen for Smiley at first lick. I knew that feeling. It had been the same for me when I first met Smooshie. However, Smooshie didn't have near the patience of Smiley. My girl could and would follow basic commands, but she'd never be "distraction proof."

When we entered the activity room, there were over a dozen residents eagerly waiting to get their hands on Smiley. And for a dog who'd spent the first year of his life on a chain without a lot of human contact, he couldn't wait for the extra love and affection. Hannah, completely in her element now, walked Smiley around to each resident and made introductions. The way the seniors lit up when Smiley put his big head on their laps brought tears to my eyes.

"Get your hands off me! I can do it myself," I heard a woman demand. The voice hadn't come from the activity room. It was fainter than that, farther away down the hall somewhere. I would have ignored it, since the woman sounded irritated, not frightened, but I recognized the voice as Opal Dixon's. Opal was one of the first people I'd met when I moved to Moonrise, an elderly woman who lived out in the country with her younger sister, Pearl, and she was someone I'd grown quite fond of over the past three years.

I tapped Annie Blankenship on the shoulder. This close, she smelled like sweat and lemon drops. "I'll be right back," I told her, trying not to wrinkle my nose at her scent.

She nodded then turned her attention back to the pet-therapy session.

I stepped out of the room and used my werecougar senses to stretch my hearing, blocking out the housekeeping staff complaining about having to clean urine that had spilled from a catheter bag, and sought to isolate Opal's speech patterns.

At the third room down the hall, I hit pay dirt.

Opal was sitting up on the side of the bed nearest the window while a frazzled-looking young woman was trying to put a shoe on Opal's right foot. Opal tried to slap the aide's hand away. "I'm going to use my good leg to put a foot up your—"

"Hey, Opal," I said, before she could finish the threat. "What are you doing here?"

"Mariah is helping her dress for lunch," the woman in the first bed said. She was a large lady with wiry gray hair, one side frizzy, the other side plastered to her head as she rolled toward me. Her right foot was uncovered, and I saw a crusted sore on the outside of her small toe. The rest of her toes were a light shade of purplish-pink. There were a few diseases that caused poor circulation, but with the woman's size and the almost sweetly alcoholic scent wafting from her direction, I was betting on uncontrolled diabetes.

"I'm getting tortured," Opal disagreed. "And I can answer for myself, Jane." Opal's glasses were nearly off her face. She pushed them up with a finger slide up the bridge of her nose and glared at her roommate. "I can also dress myself." She snatched her sock from the aide's hand. "I don't need your help."

Mariah stood up. "Suit yourself, but I can't let you get in the chair on your own. I'll get in trouble for that."

"Shoo fly," Opal said with disgust. The aide quickly got out of kicking distance.

Jane, the roommate, waved a pudgy hand at me then slid her bedside table drawer open and took out a caramel. She held it up. "Want one, honey?"

Politely, I took it and slipped it into my purse. "Thank you."

She smiled then took another one out for herself.

"My grandson brings them for me. I've always been partial to caramel chews, and he loves me."

"That's real nice," I said, not sure I meant it. If the grandson really loved her, he'd bring her some healthier treats. I looked at Opal. "So how in the world did you end up here?"

Opal forced a smile when her gaze met mine. "I broke my damn hip, kid." She pointed to her bandaged right thigh. "It's hell getting old."

"Did you get a replacement?" The bandage was a little low for a new joint.

"Land sakes. Nothing that dramatic. I broke the big bone. Doctor says I'm lucky it was a clean break near the center and not closer to my hip, otherwise it would have been a bigger surgery, and I wouldn't be allowed to put any weight on it for a month. Can you imagine me sitting around doing nothing for that long?"

There was a bead of perspiration forming on her upper lip as she grunted and cussed trying to put her sock on.

"I can't imagine it at all." Opal and Pearl were active septuagenarians. They had lunch at The Cat's Meow every day, and on Wednesdays, they went to the courthouse to see who was being charged with what crimes. It was cheap entertainment for the sisters.

I crossed the room to Opal and squatted. "I'll help her, if that's okay."

"Fine by me," Mariah said. "She's all yours."

I smirked up at my friend. "You know she's just doing her job."

"And doing it badly," Opal quipped.

I gave Mariah a sympathetic look, but she didn't seem all that mad about Opal's critique as she busied herself getting Jane sitting up on the side of the bed. Mariah put a soft boot on the woman's right foot then carefully eased it down to the floor.

I glanced at Opal's thigh after I slipped her shoe on. "How in the world did you break your leg? And why am I finding out about it by accident?"

"About four days ago." She shook her head in disgust. "Freaking trash pandas got into my garbage for the umpteenth time, and I took a broom out to chase them off. Pearl was hollering for me to go around the garbage cans while she flanked them from the front."

"Did it attack you?" I wasn't sure about regular raccoons, but raccoon-shifters liked to fight.

Opal shook her head, a faint blush of pink rising in her cheeks. "I tripped over one of Pearl's damn flamingos."

I nodded my head. Opal and Pearl's yard had at least a hundred plastic pink flamingos.

The aide, who had put a gait belt around Jane and transferred her to a wheelchair, said, "I didn't know we had flamingos in Missouri."

"Only at the zoo," Opal said. She looked at me and rolled her eyes.

"She's talking about her lawn ornaments," I told the girl. "Opal has a gazillion of them stuck around her place."

"Oh," Mariah said. "That sounds neat." She ran a brush through Jane's hair. "Is that for the groundhogs?"

Opal shook her head. "That one's not very bright."

"You know, that one can hear you, and I'm sure she doesn't get paid near enough to put up with meanness."

"Oh, I don't mind," Mariah said. "Having to stay in a nursing home sucks. Sometimes the only joy some of these folks get is giving me a hard time. I know it's not about me. Besides, if I ever go into a nursing home, I plan to be the meanest bitch in the manor."

Opal laughed. "Maybe I misjudged you."

"Ms. Dixon," the blonde nurse Abby said as she knocked on the open door. "Are you giving Mariah a hard time?" The nurse waved at the girl.

"She's fine," the aide said.

Abby gave her a nod of approval. "When you're done with Mrs. Davidson, Mr. Hoeffer has his call light on. Why don't you go see what's going on with him? I'll finish up with Ms. Dixon." To Mrs. Davidson, she said, "Is that a candy wrapper I see on your stand, Jane? Your blood sugar was through the roof earlier."

"It's sugar-free. Michael makes them for me special," Mrs. Davidson said in her defense.

Abby frowned. "I know. But your sugar is high today, and even sugar-free candies can raise your glucose levels. And after yesterday's incident in the craft room, I want you to be extra vigilant."

"That was a fluke," Mrs. Davidson said.

"Your blood sugar was six hundred and seventy-six, Jane. That's too many cupcakes, and..." Abby shook her head. "I don't know. But until I can figure it out, no more candy until you've had lunch and I've rechecked, okay? You have an ulcer on your foot, which is why you're getting skilled care. If your diabetes was still managed, that wouldn't have happened."

"Fine," she said like a scolded child. "I've been a diabetic my whole life. I think I know what I can and can't have, but no more candy before you've had a chance to check me again. Promise." Mrs. Davidson cast a sideways glance at me and winked.

I snickered. I had a feeling Mrs. Davidson was going to do whatever she wanted to do, when she wanted to do it.

Mariah gestured to Opal. "Ms. Dixon has the gait belt on already."

"Thanks," Abby said.

Mariah spritzed Jane's hair with a finishing spray. "There," she said. "Looking good, Mrs. Davidson," she said. "Ready to go to the activity room? They have a cute dog up there for you to pet?"

"Oh, yes," Jane replied. "That sounds fun."

After Mariah and Jane left, Abby grinned at Opal. "Don't chase off my aides, Grouchy. I have a good bunch right now, and I want to keep them."

"If they're good then they won't be chased off by the likes of me. I'm easy."

I snorted.

"Hush now," Opal said to me. She smirked. "An old lady has to have her fun."

Abby laughed. "And no one has fun like Opal Dixon."

"Do you two know each other? I mean, outside the nursing home?"

"You caught us." Abby gave me a conspiratorial

grin. "Opal and my gram were friends. Opal gave me my first drink."

I pressed my fingertips to my chest in mock shock. "How old were you?"

"Seven years old."

My mouth dropped a little in real shock at the age.

Opal cackled. "It was the tiniest sip of elderberry wine Ella had made. Not even enough to get a pissant drunk."

Abby laughed. "True. But I remember it made me feel very grown up." She leaned over and kissed Opal on the cheek. "You and Gram always had a way of making me feel special. Important."

Opal's gaze grew distant. "Ella had that effect on everyone."

Abby nodded. "I miss her, too."

"How long ago did she die?" I asked.

"Eight years now," Abby said. "Still feels like yesterday sometimes."

A knock at the door drew our attention. Paula Jackson was standing just outside the room. "Abby, you have a phone call at the desk."

"Thanks," she said. "I guess that's my cue."

"I'm Lily, by the way."

"Abby."

I gestured at her badge and smiled. "I figured. I'm glad Opal's in such good hands."

Abby nodded. "I better go. Could be a doctor or a family member. Neither of them likes to be kept waiting."

"I bet," I said. After she left, I turned back to Opal. "Did you choose this place because of her?"

"You're quite the detective, Lily Mason."

"She seems really nice."

"Abby's a good girl. Terrible taste in men. But a good girl all the same. After Ella died, we stayed close."

I looked around the small, crowded room. "What does Pearl think about all this?"

"She's ready for me to come home. She hates coming here. I think she's worried I'm going to die or something. I try to tell her it's temporary. The doctor said I only need about two weeks of rehab, and I can already walk the length of the hall and back before it starts hurting too much, but you know Pearl."

"I'll check on her, and I'll get Buzz and Parker to do it as well." Uncle Buzz had gotten back from California a week ago, where he and Nadine Booth, one of my best friends and a sheriff's deputy, had gone to see a therianthrope fertility specialist who had been making strides in cross-species mating. In other words, he had figured out how to make human-shifter babies. Buzz had gone the requisite four months without shifting and suffered all the ups and downs that came with ignoring our second nature—lack of control and severe mood swings being the biggies—in order for them to have a child together.

They hadn't said much about the trip since their return, and I didn't press them. Whatever they'd learned, Buzz had started shifting on the full moon again. I really hoped that the fertility clinic hadn't been a complete failure, but I can't say I was sorry he'd started shifting into cougar form again.

Regardless of anything else going on in his life, Buzz would still want to help the Dixon sisters. Of that, I was certain.

I could see relief soften the lines around Opal's eyes. "It sure would be a load off my mind."

I put my hand on her shoulder and was surprised at how fragile and bony it felt. "I'll be sure to come and visit you, too, until you're back at home. I better get back to Hannah and Smiley in the rec room. You should come down."

"Another time," Opal said.

I walked down the hall toward the activity room. A dark-haired woman I recognized stood in front of a rolling cart, reading a flip chart as she popped pills out of a bubble card into small cups.

"Lacy?"

Lacy Evans startled at the sound of her name. She looked up at me, not exactly friendly, but not with any real animosity. We would never be close, but the young single mother had done a lot of growing up since I'd first arrived in Moonrise. Her mother, Freda, worked for Buzz at the diner, and she'd told me that Lacy had passed the entrance exams for the LPN (licensed practical nursing) program at Two Hills Community College. I knew she'd been taking some classes since we'd both passed our GED, but I hadn't run into her in months.

"Hi, Lily," she said, then immediately turned her attention back to the chart.

Silly girl. I wasn't so easily deterred. "Your mom says you got into the nursing program. Congratulations."

She smiled. "I did. I just started the program. Moonrise Manor is going to help me pay for the classes. All I have to do is give them a two-year commitment to work as a charge nurse. I got my CMT, certified medication technician, a few weeks ago." She beamed with pride.

"That's great, Lacy. I'm so glad to hear you're doing well." After she'd been fired as Jock Simmons' secretary, money had been tight, according to Freda. Lacy had had to move out of her house and into a small apartment in town.

"Thanks."

"How's Paulie doing?" Paulie was her son, a child born out of an affair Lacy'd had with a married man. A man who turned out to be a murderer.

"Paulie's great. He's starting to talk in full sentences now. He's really smart."

"Just like his mom," I said. Lacy was intelligent, even if she didn't always act it, and the kindness cost me nothing.

She smiled at the compliment then put her hand on the chart. "Well, I best get back to work."

I nodded. "Don't let me hold you up. It's nice to see you."

When I arrived at the activity room door, Hannah and Smiley were putting smiles on everyone's faces. It never ceased to amaze me what the unconditional acceptance and love of a dog could do for people of all ages. I swear some of the folks in the room looked younger and more vital than when I'd left.

Abby sat at the nurses' station desk, still on the phone. She looked distressed.

"I understand," she said, her face red and pinched. "Yes. Yes, I understand. The doctor thinks it's necessary. I'm sorry." Pause. "She won't even have to leave. We will do it on site. I'm…I'm sorry you feel that way."

She must have caught me watching from the corner of her eye because she glanced in my direction with an apologetic smile. I nodded and headed into the activity room, gladder than ever that I chose a veterinarian path and not a nurse's life.

CHAPTER 2

The next afternoon, Parker Knowles, my part-time boss and full-time boyfriend, poured me a glass of iced tea while Smooshie, my all-of-the-time furbaby, rammed her giant head between my knees and demanded butt scratches. I had Saturday off, for once, and we'd spent most of the morning in bed. When my stomach growled louder than the dog's, we decided we'd better get up before my body started eating itself.

"Poor Opal," Parker said. "Must be hard for her to give up her independence, even if only for a short time." He laid out eight pieces of bread and began to liberally smear mayonnaise on them.

"I'd say two weeks is more than a short time." I lifted the glass out of the way and set it on the dining room table when Smooshie brought her head up into my lap.

"You almost wore it," Parker said. The corner of his mouth quirked up. "She adores you." He stacked ham on four of the eight pieces, added some bacon he'd fried up first, and then covered them with thick tomato slices.

I placed my hands on either side of Smooshie's jowls and kissed the top of her nose. "I adore her."

He completed the sandwiches and cut them diagonally, then put six halves on my plate and two on his own.

"You got any more of those kisses for me?" He put the plate in front of me then sat on the chair next to mine and leaned in for a smooch. I obliged him, pressing my lips against his with a sweet kiss that promised more heat later. His half smile turned into a full-blown grin. "It's nice. The two of us like this."

"I agree," I said. Parker and I spent most days and nights together, enough that he had a drawer in my trailer, and I had two at his place.

"I have more ham if you want another sandwich."

I took a bite, my stomach protesting when I didn't immediately gobble the rest down. "I may need more." I giggled. "I worked off a lot of calories last night."

"We sure did." He took my hands in his. "And we should really think about making our situation more permanent."

We'd had this conversation before. As much as I wouldn't have minded living with Parker, I liked having my own space out in the country. My fixer-upper house was nearly livable, and the ten acres it sat on was wooded enough for me to shift into my cougar form whenever I wanted. I lived for that freedom, especially since I worked two jobs, carried a full load of classes, and was trying to have a life on top of all of it. "You know I can't move to town."

He tucked one of my loose curls behind my ears. His touch, as always, raised a longing in me.

"I like how nervous you get when I talk about us living together. It's cute." He said it in a way that was meant to be teasing, but I could see how much I hurt him every time I said no.

"I'm sorry."

He stood, and Elvis, his Great Dane-pit bull mix, got up from a mat near the back door and walked over to stand next to him. Smooshie took the opportunity to flank the mammoth dog and sniff his butt. Elvis whacked her across the face with his lethal tail. She jumped back and looked at me.

I shrugged. "That's what happens when you stick your big nose where it doesn't belong."

Parker chuckled.

"What?"

"I think sticking her nose where it doesn't belong runs in the family."

I laughed. "*Touché.*" Not minding my own business had gotten me into plenty of trouble since I'd moved to Moonrise. "But I've turned over a new leaf." If I never had another mystery to solve it would be too soon. "I'm just an average college student trying to earn her way through academia."

"Who changes into a cougar and occasionally gets to hang out with witches." His face lit up when he said it.

"That too," I agreed. A few months back, I'd taken Parker to my best friend Hazel's wedding. To say things got explosive was putting it mildly. Parker had put himself in the thick of the action, and we'd taken down a homicidal warlock together. I worried the episode would trigger his PTSD, but he'd taken the whole fight in stride. "But I'm avoiding violence and dead bodies from now on."

He dipped down and kissed my forehead. "I love you."

He said it often, but still, my heart did a little back-flip every time I heard the words. "I love you, too." I smiled. "Hey, do you want to go with me to visit Opal? Buzz is going to see Pearl today and take her some reheatable dinners. I want to let Opal know so she won't worry about her sister."

Opal Dixon—a last name I was certain didn't belong to her or Pearl—had left Vegas under murky circumstances. Opal had shot Pearl's husband for beating her sister, and then they'd absconded with all the money in his safe. Unfortunately, that money had belonged to the mob. Moonrise had become the sisters' version of witness protection. Pearl didn't seem frail at all, but Opal worried about her. I couldn't blame her. I knew what it was like to feel responsible for a younger sibling. I only wished I could have saved Danny the way Opal had saved Pearl.

"I'd like to, but I can't. I'm meeting a couple looking to adopt at the shelter in an hour."

"I thought you were taking the day off."

"I am." He smiled. "Mostly."

"Besides, you want to check on Dave, right?"

"You know me so well."

Dave was a new pup we'd taken on, and his progress had been slower than either of us liked. "I can go with you. We can go see Opal after," I said hopefully.

Parker nodded. "That works for me." He hesitated. "Theresa is working today."

I sighed. "I know. We can be in the same room together. We're still friends. Just taking a small break, is all." Although, by my estimation, four months was a pretty big break.

When her husband was killed back in May, Theresa Simmons' father, the ex-sheriff of Moonrise, had tried to railroad my uncle Buzz on a bogus murder charge, all to protect his daughter and cover up his wife's shady business deals that involved illegal gambling and local government corruption. And because of my investigation, Sheriff Avery had lost his job, and he and his wife had barely escaped a prison sentence.

"It's not your fault," Parker said. "Sheriff Avery got off lucky." Anger flared in his eyes. "As far as I'm concerned, he should be rotting in a jail cell."

Did I mention that Avery pulled a gun on me? And because of his bungling of the case, the real killer almost turned *me* into another victim.

I didn't blame Theresa for wanting distance from me. When my parents were killed, through no fault of their own, I couldn't stand the way the townsfolk in Paradise Falls looked at me. Like I was an animal to be pitied. The people in Moonrise viewed Theresa much the same. Since her dad had been an elected official, there wasn't a single place in the community where Theresa could escape his notoriety. On top of that, she was a six-month-pregnant widow, and the father of the baby wasn't her dead ex, but a younger man she'd been having an affair with for the past two or three years.

The events surrounding the Averys and the Simmonses would give gossipmongers something to talk about for years to come.

"I'll take the dogs out if you want to jump in the shower." I'd showered when Parker had gone to the kitchen to get lunch started.

He sniffed his arms. "Do I smell bad?"

"Never," I told him. Honestly, he smelled of honey and mint all the time, thanks to our mate bond. "You could roll around in pig poop and you'd still smell delicious."

"I'll bear that in mind the next time I hang out with pigs." He kissed me. "You could join me if you were of a mind to."

I wrapped my arms around his waist. "I am totally of a mind to."

THE NEW RESCUE SHELTER WAS FINALLY COMPLETE, BUT THE place still needed monthly donations for utilities, food, medical procedures and medicines, toys, and hygiene stuff like shampoo, laundry detergent, and so on. We'd also had a lot of storms lately, and Theresa had put thunder vests at the top of our want-list on the website. Some of the dogs we saved reacted badly to loud noises and the vests help to soothe their nerves. I'd read some-where that CBD oil could help with extreme stress, but I wanted to study it some more before I brought it up to Parker. He'd made me a partner at the rescue since I'd donated a big portion of the money for construction, but I didn't feel comfortable making big decisions about new treatments for the dogs without running it by him first.

After we pulled in, I took Smooshie around back to one of the fenced-in play areas. She was a lovable ball of energy who liked to be the center of attention. In other words, she would try to steal the spotlight from the dogs up for adoption, and she was so cute, she would probably succeed. I'm biased when it comes to Smooshie, though, so maybe not, but there was no sense in taking chances.

Parker had gone inside without me. Elvis, his pupper, knew how to behave with company. PTSD service dogs, like all service dogs, go through extensive training for more than a year, and it had cost Parker a pretty penny. Elvis and the comfort he brought Parker made him worth every last cent.

I'd been trying to train Smooshie on basic commands, and she had gotten pretty good at sit and stay, as long as I was looking at her. The moment I'd turn my back is the moment she stopped sitting and staying.

I walked into the shelter after putting Smooshie out to play, the hall smelling faintly of bleach. I peeked into the open office door before entering. Theresa sat at the desk, diligently working on the website. She had inherited all of her husband's property, money, investments, and she'd even benefited from a generous life insurance payout, so she didn't have to work. She had given up her paid position, and she'd made a sizeable donation to the center from the sale of Jock's house.

Even so, she'd insisted on staying as long as Parker wanted her there. He'd been grateful for her generous donation and offer, and he accepted it, as long as Theresa agreed to stay a board member. She had. Thanks to her money and efforts, we could pay the basic bills without any more money coming in if times got hard.

I was just glad we had enough money to take on some of the tougher rescues, where a lot of expensive medical care was necessary. Our latest rescue, Dave, a brindle pit bull, tall like a mastiff, had been found tied to a tree in the woods two counties north of us, severely emaciated, a horrible infection in his right eye, and both ears had been damaged, most likely from fights. Ryan Petry, my other boss, and the local veterinarian, had given us antibiotics and drops for Dave's eye, but he didn't have a lot of hope it would heal on its own. Chances were, Dave was going to need to have his eye removed.

It was stories like Dave's that made me question humanity. However, watching the valiant efforts of the volunteers and foster families reminded me that most people were good at their core, and that, like apples, one rotten person didn't spoil the bunch.

I had only seen Theresa a handful of times over the past few months, so I was surprised to see how far her belly stuck out while she was seated. She pivoted her chair toward me and caught me looking.

She put her hand on top of the curve. "Getting big," she said.

"You look great," I said and wasn't lying or embellishing the truth. Her skin was luminescent. It would be cliché to say she had a pregnancy glow, because I'd seen some pregnant women whose skin looked like it had been hammered by a meat tenderizer, but in Theresa's case it was true. "Being pregnant suits you."

Her smile warmed. "Thanks, Lily. Where's Smoosh?"

"I put her in the north play area.

She looked past me as Parker entered the room. "The Meyers will be here soon. Keith has got Dot, Bean Blossom, Sweet Pea, and Carly ready to show them," she said to him.

I gave her a curious look after she'd listed off the names.

"They want to adopt a female," Theresa said.

"Is Dot ready for adoption?" Dot had been struggling with her training classes.

"She passed her good citizen's test yesterday," Parker said. He draped his arm across my shoulder. "I meant to tell you last night, but after you finished telling me about Opal, I forgot."

"Opal?" Theresa asked. "What's going on with her?"

I didn't see any harm in sharing Opal's situation. "She broke her hip. She's at the Moonrise Manor nursing home to get the rehab she needs to get back on her feet. I've organized some people to check in on Pearl and visit Opal so neither of them gets lonely."

"Pearl drives, right? So, she can go visit her sister."

"I'm not sure. Maybe." I'd only ever seen Opal behind the wheel of their older model Mercury. "We're going to visit Opal after the Meyers leave. I'll make sure and ask." If Pearl didn't drive, then we would have to make sure she had someone to take her to see Opal daily until she was discharged.

"Well, if you need any help taking up the slack either here or with the Dixon sisters, you let me know."

"I'll take you up on it." My throat tightened. This was the longest conversation I'd had with Theresa since everything had gone down in May. I tried not to show too much excitement about the fact that she was having a real conversation with me because I was afraid that if I made any kind of deal about it, I'd remind her that she was still unhappy with me.

"Good," Theresa said. "I hope you will." She scooted away from us and back to the desk. She wiggled her computer mouse to wake up the screen.

Parker gently squeezed my shoulder, a gesture of reassurance. "Let's go check on Dave before they get here."

Dave was sitting at the far end of one of our isolation kennels for sick pups, on the large, blanket-covered cot. He'd cleaned his food bowl and was low on water. "His appetite is back," I said with no small amount of satisfaction. "That's a good sign." Dave had been reluctant to eat when he'd first arrived. Ryan had found an abscessed tooth on his initial exam, so he'd removed it. Dave's mouth had been sore for a few days, but the fact that he was eating now meant he was on the mend.

"Yeah," Parker agreed. "But his eye is still about the

same. No improvement since we put him on antibiotics two days ago." We'd been putting it in his food, and he'd been too hungry to care.

Dave's swollen right eye was crusty with matter. It needed cleaning, but that wasn't going to happen until Dave trusted us to get close. "He'll probably need surgery."

"I hate for him to lose his eye," Parker said. "But I think you're right."

I opened the door to his kennel and ducked inside. Parker closed it behind me. I sat cross-legged on the floor a few feet from Dave, held out a treat, and waited for him to respond. He whimpered at first, his way of saying drop the tasty and leave, but I shook my head. "It's all right, boy. No one's going to hurt you. Not anymore."

Dave was having a hard time trusting people, and who could blame him. Ryan had guesstimated his age to be around four years, which meant he'd most likely *suffered* for four years before some asshole had tied him to that tree to starve to death.

"He'll get there, Lils," Parker said.

"I know." Even though I didn't. Some animals, like some people, were too broken to fix, but I comforted myself with the fact that Dave would never want for a meal, a safe place to run, and a roof over his head for the rest of his life.

I froze as Dave gingerly stepped down from the cot and held my breath as he stretched his neck until his lips moved against the edge of the dog biscuit. I couldn't see Parker, but I could feel his stillness behind me.

The biscuit fell from my hand, and with a quickness I hadn't seen in the dog, he snatched it from the ground and chomped it like a last meal on his way back to the safety of his cot. I looked back at Parker, whose grin mirrored my own.

"Progress," he said.

I cast my gaze back to Dave. "You're a good boy. Such a good boy." His tail didn't flicker, and his eyes still held suspicion, but he'd taken food from my hand, and I counted that a win.

A rap on the window to the isolation room drew our attention. It was Keith. "The Meyers are here," he said through the door.

CHAPTER 3

G eri and Frank Meyer were a married middle-aged couple. Geri was a pharmacist and Frank, a retired naval officer. It was a second marriage for both of them. Geri's daughter worked in financing in St. Louis, and Frank's boys lived with their mother in California, but he had moved back to Moonrise after his divorce because his father had fallen ill. They'd been married for two years, and, until recently, Geri had owned a pit bull female named Bizzy, who had died of heart failure at the age of thirteen.

I knew all this in the first ten minutes of their arrival because Geri liked to talk. I didn't discount the fact that my inherited witch gifts made me more susceptible to TMI from friends and strangers.

Parker had vetted them a week ago before approving their adoption. They'd lost Bizzy eight months earlier, and Geri was ready to love again.

Dot, a brown American bully type—which meant she had a stocky, muscular body, and a head nearly as wide as her chest—barreled into the room, nearly knocking me over to hug against my leg. Unfortunately, she was more interested in Parker and me than the Meyers. Bean Blossom was a pit bull-beagle mix, and she was more attentive to the couple. Carly, another bully, with a light caramel-colored coat, also showed herself to be a sweet cuddle-monkey.

But when Sweet Pea, a black and white French bull-dog-pit mix, got her turn, I knew it was over. Geri and Frank both lit up when they saw her, and Sweet Pea quickly squirmed her way onto their laps and into their hearts.

After all the paperwork had been filled out, adoption fees collected, and pictures for the website and social media taken, it was after two-thirty.

"We should get going to Moonrise Manor," I said to Parker.

Frank overheard me. "Moonrise Manor? Do you have family there?"

"A friend. She broke her leg and needs some physical therapy."

"My father is a resident over there," Frank said. "He's been there for the past two years."

"I'm sorry."

"It was a difficult decision, but in the end, the best one for the family."

"So, you like the place?"

"They do a good job." He hesitated, then said, "Mostly."

"Mostly?"

"Well, there was an incident three months ago.

Some of his pain pills went missing. We probably wouldn't have known anything about it, but Geri's pharmacy supplies the nursing home. They had to order Dad's pills early. Insurance wouldn't pay on an early refill, so we ended up having to cover the cost out of pocket."

"What did the manor say about the discrepancy?"

Frank shrugged. "Improper disposal. One of the nurses came forward and said she'd dropped the pills on a dirty floor after I complained. She said she disposed of them and meant to chart it after her med pass but forgot. Needless to say, the manor footed the final bill on the replacements."

"Wow."

"It happens," he said.

An excited bark from Sweet Pea drew his attention. She and his wife Geri were standing in the open front door, waiting on Frank. "I better go," he said. "I hope your friend recovers quickly."

When they left out the front, Parker came over and put his arm around me. "You ready to get out of here?"

"I am."

THE NURSING HOME WAS SOLEMN WHEN WE ARRIVED AT A little after three in the afternoon, not the hub of activity it had been on Friday. I heard televisions on in several rooms, some quiet whispers, too far and too low for me to make out the conversation, along with sniffling that accompanied tears.

All the joy I'd felt about the adoption seeped out of me.

Parker nudged my shoulder. "What's wrong?"

"Opal. I can hear her…I think she's crying."

We picked up our pace, passing the abandoned nurses' station at a fast clip. Her door was open, and I grazed the wood, an attempted knock, as I barreled inside the room.

Opal was in a wheelchair, a box of tissues in her lap. Her roommate's bed was empty.

"Are you okay?" I asked.

She glanced up at me, her red-rimmed eyes filled with pain. "She's gone."

I looked at Jane Davidson's bed. The nurse had wanted to get bloodwork on the woman. She had suspected something and now the old woman was dead. "I'm so sorry, Opal. Did you know her well?"

"I've known Abby her whole life," she said.

I took a moment to gather my thoughts. Opal and Pearl had come to Moonrise a little over thirty years ago. Jane Davidson had easily been in her seventies. Opal couldn't have known her that long, unless Jane had known them when they were in Vegas.

Just as I was about to ask, Mariah, the CNA from the day before, wheeled Jane into the room.

I blinked as if seeing a ghost. I knelt down in front of Opal and placed my hand over hers. "Who died?" It certainly hadn't been Jane Davidson.

Opal stared at me. "Abby."

My heart did a double flip. "The nurse?"

"Ella loved her. I loved her. She was like my very own granddaughter."

"Was she in an accident?"

Opal shook her head. She pulled a tissue out of the box and blew her nose. "They say she killed herself." She shook her head even harder. "She wouldn't."

I'd met Abby the day before. She didn't seem like a woman on the edge, but I knew what it was like to act as if everything was right as rain in public while falling apart in private. I'd done it enough trying to raise my brother after my parents died. I'd never seriously considered suicide, but it had crossed my mind, fleetingly, once or twice as a way out of my circumstances.

"Sometimes people put on a brave face," I said.

"How did she do it?" Parker asked. I gazed up at him; his expression was bleak.

"The police wouldn't tell me, but I overheard one of the aides say that she took an overdose of pills. Pills they said she might have stolen from patients." Opal shredded the tissue between her fingertips. "She wasn't that way, Lily." Her eyes narrowed. "You have to believe me. She wasn't that way." Her voice choked. "I just won't believe it."

"The police were out here?"

"This morning. They wanted to talk to anyone who worked with her yesterday. Someone told them that I was a family friend."

I knew it couldn't have been Nadine who took the call. She hadn't gone back to work yet after her return from California, but I knew she was scheduled to start again on Monday. And Buzz had finally returned to full-time cooking duties at The Cat's Meow. During his non-shifting months, Buzz had hired another waitress and a part-time cook at the diner to cover for the days when his shifter side got a little too raw for public consumption. Freda took on a more supervisory position, with a raise, to manage those days when Buzz couldn't make it in. She didn't know the circumstances behind his sudden mood swings and such, but she was willing to accept that he was going through something, and she would do what she could to help him. Still, neither Buzz nor Nadine had been acting right since their return.

"Was it Bobby Morris who talked to you?" Bobby Morris was still the acting sheriff until the coming elections. He'd stepped into Sheriff Avery's shoes without a lot of fuss, and he was a damn sight better than Avery had ever been at the job. He might have an uphill battle winning an election, but I planned to vote for him when the time came.

"No." She shook her head. "Larry Shobe was the deputy who talked to me," Opal said. "He asked me if Abby had been upset about anything personal. Abby was a happy person."

"I'm sure she was," I said. And she had seemed happy for the most part, except for when she'd been talking to the doctor, or while on the phone with whoever she'd been on the phone with. But from what little I'd seen, none of it added up to suicide. Maybe she'd been addicted to drugs and accidentally overdosed. I didn't say that out loud because it would just add to Opal's misery.

"I'm sorry you're going through this, Opal. It's hard to lose people you love."

"You can find out for me, right? You know how awful the cops are around here. They'll say Abby's death is open and shut, and no one will try to find the truth."

"Is there a reason you suspect someone might have done this to her? Did she say something to you?" I asked.

Opal knocked her tissue box onto the floor. "I know Abby! She wasn't the kind of girl to steal drugs, and she wasn't the kind of girl to kill herself."

A knock outside the door drew our attention. Annie Blankenship, the activity director, stepped into the room. "I'm going to have a group bereavement session today at two if you would like to come, Ms. Dixon." Annie gave the briefest of acknowledgements to Mrs. Davidson. "You too, Jane. Abby was loved by a lot of people, and we're all going to miss her."

Opal grabbed an empty plastic pudding container from her bedside stand and flung it in Annie's direction. "Get out of here, you ghoul!"

"Opal!" I said. "This isn't Annie's fault." I looked at the activity director, who'd gone several shades pale. "Please don't be angry with her. Opal has known Abby for a long time. She's just in shock."

Annie nodded quickly. "I'll check back later." She glanced over at Mrs. Davidson. "What about you, Jane?"

"I don't want to go," the elderly woman said. She gave Annie a baleful stare. "Please don't ask again."

"I understand," Annie said. She gave me a nod then left.

I felt bad for her. The activity director was basically the morale police in a place, trying to bring joy and a sense of well-being to folks who were often miserable. It wasn't the care center's fault. It was just a byproduct of aging in humans. Sometimes, a person got to a point where they just couldn't take care of themselves anymore. That loss of independence would be enough to depress anyone. Something like losing a beloved caregiver was bound to make her job with the residents a thousand times harder.

I took Opal's hands. "What can I do for you? Just tell me, and I'll try my best to help you through this," I said as a helplessness filled me. Abby's death had taken a toll on Opal, and she looked ten years older than she had the day before.

She gave me a sharp-eyed stare. "You can do what you do. Nose around. Investigate. You've solved several murders in this town before. What's one more?"

"This isn't a murder," I said gently. Even if it had been, I was out of the tracking-down-killers business.

"Then it won't cost you anything to ask around," she said bluntly. "I'll pay you." She grabbed my hand and pulled me closer. "You know I have the money."

"I couldn't and wouldn't take your money, Opal." I glanced at Parker. His thoughts looked far off, his eyes darting back and forth as if he were reliving an unpleasant memory. I stood up and ran my hand down his arm. His stare became less wild, more present. But his reaction, along with Opal's assertations, prompted me to do something I'd sworn I'd stop doing. Getting involved.

Finally, I nodded. "What's Abby's last name?"

"Rogers," Opal said.

"I'll ask around," I promised.

The relief in her eyes worried me. Chances were Abby committed suicide. If it walked like a duck, simplest explanation is usually the right one, and all that. "I can't make this into something it's not," I told her. "If it turns out she really did kill herself, are you going to be able to accept that as an answer?"

Opal nodded, then said, "Probably not."

My back stiffened until Parker laced his fingers with mine. This was the kind of thing that could sever a friendship. Opal wanted the answer she wanted, whether evidence supported her beliefs or not. Most people, I found, were like that. "I can only go where evidence and facts take me."

Opal frowned. "I know that." She glanced at the door. "I'm going to go stir-crazy sitting around here. How about if you bust me out of this place, and I can do a little digging around myself?"

"How about if we save the digging for Smooshie?" I softened my words with a sympathetic smile. "Besides, it seems to me you're in the perfect place to find out stuff about what happened to Abby. You can conduct your own investigation here at the manor, and I'll see what I can learn on the outside. I'll come back on Monday or Tuesday and we'll compare notes."

Opal fake-spat in her hand and held it out to me. "Deal," she said.

I nodded, faked spitting in my own hand, and we shook on it. "Deal."

"You should talk to my Michael," Jane Davidson said. "He and Abby dated sometimes."

"Your son?" I asked.

"Grandson," she said. "He's a good boy, and he was fond of Abby."

I remembered Opal saying the day before that Abby had terrible taste in men. I wondered if Michael was one of those men. I didn't ask, because I didn't want to upset Jane. Instead, I nodded. "Do you have his details? I'll see if he's willing to talk to me."

"I have his card." Jane used her feet to propel her to the candy drawer. Inside were a slew of empty wrappers. She dug around until she found what she was looking for. A small, worn business card with frayed sides. "Here."

I took it from her. "Michael Lowell," I read. "Website Consultant." A phone number and email address were under the job title.

"He teaches kindergarten full-time, but he has always been good with computers," Jane said. "He does the consulting part-time."

"Thanks." I tucked the card in my back pocket and looked at Opal. "Do you need anything else?"

"Just find out what happened to Abby," she said.

Before we left the room, I remembered Theresa's question. "Can Pearl drive, or do we need to arrange rides for her to visit you?"

"Pearl can drive, but she doesn't like to."

"Then we'll get a carpool going for her," I said.

"You really are thoughtful, Lily," Opal said as fresh tears fell down her cheeks.

Parker's fingers clinched around mine. He was not handling the visit well at all. We probably should have brought Elvis along.

I wrapped my arm around his waist, touching him with as much of my body as the position would allow. Unconsciously, he began stroking my hair with his other hand. I could hear his heartbeat and breathing slow.

We said our goodbyes, and I promised Opal I would tell her if I found out anything new about her friend. As Parker and I walked down the hall, the tension eased from his muscles as he continued to play with my hair.

I glanced up at him. "You okay?"

"Yeah," he said. "Just brought up some stuff for me I'd sooner forget."

"You want to talk about it?"

He shook his head. "Not now."

"I just met Abby yesterday. She was nice. Funny. Bubbly, even."

"Drug addicts can take all shapes. A lot of them live functional lives."

"I know."

"Your brother?"

"Yep." Although, Danny had only become functional once he'd quit the hard drugs. "I wish I could have said no to Opal."

"Chances are Abby's death will be exactly what they

suspect," Parker said.

"They'll have to do an autopsy. I'll talk to Reggie." My friend, Regina Crawford, was a general practitioner doctor in town, but also the medical examiner. Abby would have to pass through Reggie's capable hands before a final determination of suicide. "That's a good place to start."

Lacy Evans was inside the medication room behind the nurses' station. Three lights flashed on the wall, room numbers underneath them.

Mariah, the aide, hurried toward us looking frazzled.

"Busy day," I said as she passed.

"I'm the only aide on this hall today. The other two called in sick, and they can't find anyone to replace them."

Lacy poked her head out of the room. "I'll help as soon as I get the meds passed," she said. She looked almost as haggard as the aide. She nodded to Parker and me, her eyes red like Opal's had been. "Abby was supposed to work today. I'm covering what I can until they can find an evening shift replacement. But it's Saturday, so I'm not holding my breath."

"Were you friends with Abby?"

"Not outside of work, but I liked her well enough," Lacy said. "She was fair, and she cares…cared about the residents. That's not always the case around here." She looked around as if afraid someone important might hear her complain. "I better get back to it or Mariah is going to quit, then I'll be the only one on the floor."

I wanted to ask her some questions about the

missing narcotics. As a CMT, she would be in a position to know what was missing, and how much.

Before I could, though, Parker put his arm around me. "We won't hold you up," he said and steered me toward the hall leading to the front entrance.

When we made it outside, his whole body sagged in relief.

"Sorry," I told him. I knew he'd been itching to get out.

"No, I'm sorry, Lily. I don't think I can go back there."

"You don't have to," I said. "Pearl will need some company and folks to drive her around if you want to help. You don't have to go back in there."

He nodded, his expression bleak.

"When's your next appointment with the psychologist?"

Parker gave me a startled look then smiled. "You really do know me well. Wednesday at two." He hugged me. "I'll be fine. Just the news of the suicide, the wheelchairs, the smell, all of it just took me back to a time I wish I could forget."

"Do you mind dropping me off at my place? I think I'm going to drive out to see Pearl. Just to check on her."

"Of course," Parker said. "You want me to keep Smooshie at my place? You can pick her up after."

I loved that I didn't have to ask and rewarded Parker with a kiss.

He caressed my cheek. "I do like the way you say yes."

CHAPTER 4

I t was after five by the time I arrived at Pearl and Opal's place. I drove down the rough gravel drive. It had several bare spots, along with some potholes, that needed filling. It cracked me up every time I passed the plastic palm trees lining the last fifty or so feet of the driveway. Opal's sedan was parked under a three-sided carport, a newer addition to the Dixon property. The leaves on the surrounding trees had started to turn the warm colors of fall, creating an idyllic portrait of rural country living.

A white picket fence bordered the front yard along with the flock of pink flamingo lawn ornaments. The one with the broken beak and a duct-taped neck near the trash can made me smile. It might have taken Opal down, but it looked like she got some revenge on the offending fowl.

Colorful lights hung over the top of the fenced yard in a canopy of green wires with hanging yellow, red, green, and blue bulbs. I tapped the signpost pointing south that said, "Miami, 1,095 miles," when I walked up to the white fifty-foot double-wide trailer.

I knocked on the door. When Pearl didn't answer, I knocked harder. "Pearl," I said loudly. "Pearl? It's Lily. Are you in there?"

I closed my eyes and listened for any noise. I could hear Frank Sinatra singing "You Make Me Feel So Young," along with the spray and patter sounds of a shower. What else? There was a noise... Like a screech combined with a moan. The sound someone might make if they were in pain. Was Pearl hurt? Had she fallen in the shower?

I tried the door. It was unlocked. I raised my voice. "Pearl. It's Lily! I'm coming in."

The music was louder now, and so was the underlying noises. Some of them sounded almost inhuman. I charged in, narrowly missing one of their wicker chairs that was blocking access to the hall. "Pearl!"

The bathroom door was open, the Sinatra tune was blaring from a speaker on the sink counter. The shower curtain was closed, but the noise had taken on a frantic, almost panicked cadence.

I threw the curtain back.

A naked older man sat on the shower chair, and Pearl, also naked, was straddling him, their bodies clasped in full-on coitus.

I yelped. Pearl screamed, grabbing the edge of the curtain and yanking it closed between us.

"What in tarnation?" the man said.

"I'm sorry! So sorry." I babbled more apologies as I scrambled from the steamy room. My heart beat a mile a minute. I stumbled into the living room. That's when I noticed the pair of men's blue jeans on the couch, the white boxers on the coffee table, the two wine glasses, the cheese platter…

Cripes. Pearl was having a date, and I had barreled in like a pit bull in a sausage smokehouse.

Pearl walked into the room wearing her glasses now and a robe. She scowled at me.

I grimaced. "Sorry," I said again.

She plucked up the jeans, the boxers, a white T-shirt from behind the couch, and a light-blue button-down shirt from the chair near the hallway.

Dang. "That must have been some good wine."

Pearl pinned me with a gaze that could wilt flowers. "Make yourself at home," she said, "you know, since you let yourself in."

I pulled out one of the stools from the breakfast bar and sat down on the edge, my feet pointed to the door and ready to run if any household objects were thrown in my direction. About five minutes later, Pearl came back down the hall, her pink-tinted hair towel dried with the curls picked out, and she now wore a pair of white loafers, pink capris pants, and a pale-green blouse.

She crossed her arms over her chest. "What in the world are you doing here, Lily?"

"I…well, I just wanted to check in on you. Make sure you were okay. You know, not lonely."

Her gaze softened. "I'm fine. And, as you saw, not lonely."

The man came down the hall tucking his shirt into

his jeans. With clothes on, I recognized the tall, thin, gray-haired man as Bob Tolliver, a retired farmer who had started frequenting The Cat's Meow Diner about six months earlier.

"Hello, Lily," he said, avoiding eye contact with me. He grabbed a billed cap from an end table and put it on. He cast a slow smile at Pearl. "Walk me out."

"You don't have to go on my account," I said. "I can come back later."

Pearl gave me a stern look. "You," she said, punctuating the word with a pointed finger. "Wait right there."

I did as I was told. Pearl wasn't nearly as thin as Opal, but she had a pleasant shape. By the way Bob was looking at her, I could tell he thought so, too.

They left, and when Pearl finally came back inside, her cheeks were flushed. "You have the worst timing, Lily Mason."

I tried not to laugh, and my effort turned into a snort. "I really do." I moved the curtain aside and glanced out the window. I saw a white pickup truck heading up the drive. I hadn't seen it when I pulled up. "Where was he parked?"

"On the other side of the carport." She shook her head.

"So, you're dating Bob Tolliver, huh?"

She *psshed* me. "People my age don't date."

I pointed to the wine glasses. "What do you call it?"

"Bob and I have been special friends going on a few months," she said unapologetically.

"If I had known you'd have company, I would have called ahead. I could have avoided the nasty flamingo."

I made a circle with my thumb and index finger then poked it with my other index finger. It was a gesture she liked to use when using the phrase in conjunction with everyone else's love lives, and it was fun to throw it back at her.

"Hah!" She laughed. "Bob's wife died a year ago, and he's not ready for his kids to know he's socializing again. So, we're, how do you kids say it, keepin' it on the down-low."

"I'm going to buy you a stuffed flamingo to hang on the doorknob when your entertaining company."

"Or you could just call ahead," Pearl said.

"That works, too." I laughed. "Personally, I think it's great you have a special friend. When I found out Opal was in the nursing home, I was worried about you. It looks like you're doing okay."

"Buzz told me you were visiting, Opal. That's really thoughtful. He brought out those dinners this morning and told me that you all would take turns visiting her. That makes me feel better. But I'm not as fragile as everyone thinks." Pearl walked over and sat on the couch. "Come have a seat."

I joined her. "Opal always just comes off as more sure of herself."

"She likes to think she's in charge, but I'm not the same woman I was when we left Vegas." Pearl gave me a meaningful look. "I know she told you about our... situation." Pearl put her hand on my arm.

"We all have pasts," I said. "Moonrise gave me a fresh start. I was able to reinvent myself, and I'm thankful for the chance at a clean slate."

"I'm not sure my slate will ever be clean, but we have the fresh start in common."

"Have you talked to Opal today?"

"On the phone. I called her this morning. She was getting ready to go to breakfast, and she got a little cranky with me. She's always grumpy before coffee."

"So, you haven't seen or talked to her since then?"

Pearl's brow furrowed. "What is it, Lily? Did something happen to Opal? Is she okay? Did she fall? Something worse?" Her words grew breathy. "Is she in the hospital? Just tell me! What's happened to my sister?"

"Nothing like that," I assured her. "Opal is okay. It's not her."

"Then who?"

"How well did you know Abby Rogers?"

"I know Abby real well. Her grandmother was a close friend to Opal. Ella doted on Abby, and when Ella died, Opal and I kept in contact with her after. Why are you asking me how well I knew her? What's happened?"

"I'm so sorry, Pearl. I hate to be the one to tell you, but Abby has died."

Her hands trembled. "What? How? She just celebrated her thirtieth birthday. How is this even possible?"

I shook my head. "I don't know. But I promised Opal I'd ask around."

"How did she die?"

"According to Opal, the police think she overdosed on narcotics."

"She didn't do the whacky tobaccy."

"I'm not sure you can OD from marijuana. I suspect it will be some kind of opioid, like hydrocodone."

Pearl shook her head emphatically. "I just can't believe that of Abby."

"Are you sure?"

Her skin had taken on a ghastly pallor that aged her beyond her seventy-something years. She nodded. "As sure as I can be about anyone who isn't living in my head."

"Do you want me to fix you some coffee? Tea?"

"There's a bottle of brandy under the sink."

The only thing separating the kitchen from the living room was a breakfast bar covered with a Formica countertop with a travel sticker design. I navigated around it to the sink and took the bottle of brandy from the space below.

"Cups are to the right," Pearl instructed. "Two fingers, please."

I unscrewed the cap on the half-empty bottle of brandy. The aroma of fermented sweet apricots burned my nostrils. Pouring enough to climb the skinny glass about an inch and a half from the base, I held it up for Pearl's approval.

"That's fine," she said. She immediately sipped it when I handed her the drink. "Abby's had her troubles. I know Opal worries about her." She took another drink. "Worried. Oh, poor Opal. She's got to be devastated."

"Why did she worry about Abby?"

"The usual." Pearl set the glass on the coffee table and wrung her hands. "Abby had terrible taste in men.

Her ex-husband, a radiologist at the hospital, had some anger issues. Abby confided in us that she'd taken comfort with a doctor friend. Dale, her ex-husband, found out, and he threatened to tell anyone who would listen if she fought him in the divorce. She ended up with nothing, not even an alimony settlement."

"How awful. I think I would have called him on his threats."

"The doctor was married. Maybe he still is. She hadn't wanted to ruin his life."

"Jane Davidson said Abby was seeing her grandson. Michael Lowell."

"I know about Michael. Abby said he was...nice. That's always the kiss of death in a new relationship."

"I think Parker's nice," I said.

Pearl sniffed then chuckled. "But that's not how you would describe him to a friend, right? You'd say things like built for dipping his crane in your turbulent waters, making the beast with two backs, doing the horizontal mambo, and—"

"The nasty flamingo?" I choked on a laugh. "Just for the record, I would never say any of that to anyone, not even a friend, but I get your point."

"I'm afraid Michael never had a real shot."

"Do you think he would have done something to Abby? Opal is sure she didn't take her own life and a spurned lover is as good a motive as it gets." People, regardless of species, could do some really awful things out of jealousy.

"Maybe. But Michael's a kindergarten teacher, for the love of Pete. I just don't see it."

"What about that doctor she was seeing?"

She shook her head. "What reason would he have to kill her?"

"Maybe she got tired of waiting for him to leave his wife?"

"As far as I know they ended things." Opal sighed her frustration. "Have you talked to that friend of yours? The one that cuts up dead bodies?"

"Reggie Crawford."

"That's the one. I'm sure glad to see Greer Knowles has a new gal pal in his life, but her profession sure is ghoulish."

"She's a regular doctor most of the time," I said in Reggie's defense.

"Well, did you talk to her? She'd be taking care of Abby, wouldn't she?"

"Not yet. I came here to check on you first."

"Well, get your pocket phone and call her. Land sakes. What kind of detective are you?"

"The kind that's not a detective," I said. But I got out my cell phone. "She might not have any results in. Final reports can take weeks."

"She strikes me as a smart cookie. I'm sure she'll have an opinion or two."

I could see I wasn't going to get away without calling Reggie before I left. I brought up my contacts and touched a picture of her sticking out her tongue at me. She always looked so put together, her clothes tailored, her hair and makeup just right, which is why I loved the picture. To me, it was the only one that really captured Reggie's personality.

The phone rang on her end. She picked up. "Hey, Lils," she answered. "What's up?"

"Hey, Reg," I said. "Did you get called about a death today? Young woman named Abby—"

"Abigail," Pearl interjected.

"—Abigail Rogers?"

Reggie was quiet for a few seconds, then said, "Please don't tell me you found her body."

"I did not find the body," I said, a little too triumphantly, but I was seriously getting tired of being called a dead body magnet. "She's a good friend of Opal Dixon's. I told her I'd ask around. She doesn't think it was an accident."

"Suicide isn't an accident," Reggie said.

"So, you think she took her own life?"

"Don't go putting words in my mouth. I'm getting ready to examine the stomach contents, and I've sent blood and urine samples out for analysis."

"Did anything look suspicious when you were called to the scene?"

"I was over at a St. Louis seminar for medical examiners when I got the call. Another doctor did the initial exam before they transported the body over to the hospital morgue."

"Okay." Well, double damn. "Do you know where she died?"

"Her bedroom at her apartment, according to the initial report. There wasn't a note, but there were a few pills that I have confirmed as oxycodone hydrochloride. I won't know if she had a lethal dose in her system until after the blood tests."

"She was found in the bedroom of her apartment?"

"Yes."

Pearl got up from the couch and wandered down the hall out of sight, but I focused on my phone call. "That's not a lot to go on."

Reggie sighed. "I'm sorry I'm not more help."

"You've been great, Reg. I appreciate your candor."

"If I learn anything else, I'll let you know."

I hung up as Pearl walked back into the living room.

I raised a brow as she held up a key.

"What's that?" I asked.

She smiled. "A spare key to Abby's apartment."

CHAPTER 5

There was no talking Pearl out of going to Abby's apartment. So, I called Parker and told him I'd be late. It was getting darker earlier, now, so we waited until closer to seven in the evening to head into town. Pearl took great care to tell me every time I needed to slow down, speed up, when there was a stop sign or traffic light, and she gave me a heads up every time a turn came up, even though I usually had my turn signal on already. By the time we arrived at the Sunset Apartment Complex, I'd never been so glad to reach a destination in all my life.

I parked on a side street in a two-hour parking space. "Give me the key."

"Why?" she asked, her fingers wrapped tightly around the key.

"I need you to stay out here in the truck. I'll be able to get in and out quicker, and hopefully without notice, if I do it alone."

"I have the key because Abby has Opal water her plants and feed her cat when she's out of town. I have every reason in the world to be in there. You don't."

It was hard to fault her logic, but I was going to try. "If it turns out her death was on account of foul play, anything we disturb in there can contaminate the crime scene."

Pearl dug into her purse and pulled out a pair of yellow, elbow-length cleaning gloves. "I've thought of that. I have a pair for you, too. Besides, I might see something in her place that you don't," she protested.

"I have very good eyes," I said. And nose and ears. Just like the big, bad wolf. Only a cougar, in my case. "I won't miss anything. Besides, I need you to keep a look-out. If anyone like the police or someone suspicious goes inside the building, honk the horn."

"How in the world am I going to know if someone looks suspicious or not? At my age, anyone under the age of fifty looks suspicious."

I glanced at her. "Uh huh."

"Present company excluded, of course." She opened the passenger door and hopped out. "Now, you can sit around and argue with yourself all night. I'm going inside that apartment."

"You're plain stubborn," I told her.

"Damn right," she told me back. Her grim-set mouth and stern eyes dared me to keep fighting her.

"Fine. You can come."

"There was never any doubt," she said, tugging her bag over her shoulder. "Let's go. It's getting close to my bedtime."

"Let's try for stealth. Okay?"

"I'm a woman over seventy. Being invisible is not a problem."

She wasn't wrong. We passed two women, one in her twenties, another in her forties, and a middle-aged couple in the hall on the way to Abby's first-floor apartment. They barely looked in our direction. I guess two women, one slight and the other elderly, didn't register as odd for any of them.

I noticed an elaborate doorbell for the apartment across from Abby's that wasn't on any of the other doors.

"Probably the old lady we passed," Pearl said when I pointed it out. "You can have them installed if you're hard of hearing. Opal wanted to get one last year, but it's not like we get a lot of visitors we don't see coming." She eyed me up and down. "Present company excluded."

"I don't know how many times I'm going to have to apologize."

"As many times as it takes. Now, come on, Nancy Drew. We have clues to find." Pearl's hand shook as she forced the key into the door.

I scanned the hallway for any onlookers, but it was empty now. "Hurry," I said.

"I'm hurrying," she said with great irritation. I heard a click, and Pearl's satisfied, "Yes." She opened the door and waved me in. "Age before beauty," she said.

I rolled my eyes but went inside. Pearl closed the door behind us and gave the lock a twist. The place was a simple one-bedroom apartment layout. The living room and kitchen were on the right, and on the left was a bathroom, closet, and bedroom. There was a litter box in the corner of the tidy living room. The scent of cat urine and feces was minimal, which meant Abby had cleaned the box in the past day or two, or it was really good kitty litter.

"Here." Pearl handed me a pair of kitchen gloves.

I frowned but took them. I slid them on, the size of them swallowing most of my arm. Pearl had a similar issue. It was almost comical, the two of us walking around with rubber gloves all the way up to our armpits.

The first thing I did was lift the litter box lid. It was clean except for a few pieces of scat. "Would someone suicidal be worried about cleaning cat poop?"

"Where is Audrey?" Pearl asked.

"Is that the cat's name?"

"Yes. She's mostly white with a black patch between her ears and little black spots over her eyes. Abby said the cat reminded her of Audrey Hepburn. That girl spent too many afternoons watching old movies with old ladies." Her expression grew melancholy as she endured the memory, a painful reminder that her young friend was gone. She wiped at her eyes with the back of her gloved hand. "Now quit messing around with cat poo and get down to finding a smoking gun."

"She wasn't shot."

"Don't sass me," Pearl said. "You know what I mean."

"Why don't you check the kitchen, and I'll tackle the bedroom."

Pearl looked like she wanted to argue with me, but then nodded. "Fine. But call me if you find anything important."

"Same," I told her.

I held my breath as I walked into the bedroom. I don't know what I was expecting, but I hadn't thought it would be a room full of cat knick-knacks and wall art. The main focal piece over the head of the bed was an oil painting of a white cat with a black spot between its ears and smaller spots over its eyes. Abby's precious Audrey. It was obvious she loved that cat.

The bed had been stripped, probably bagged by the investigators. There was some minor staining on the mattress. One dark spot about midway between the head and the foot on the right side. Old blood, maybe? I reluctantly bent down to get a good whiff of the area and was pleasantly surprised to find it was coffee, and not blood or bodily waste. It was fairly fresh as well. Who drank coffee in bed?

There was a television mounted on the wall directly across from the foot of the bed. I hadn't seen one in the living room, which meant she probably spent most of her time in her bedroom. Burgundy and royal blue blackout curtains covered the windows. There was a bookshelf in the corner of the room with a small but comfortable-looking blue reading chair. Next to the chair was a cat tree with several tiers and small cubes with cutouts going almost all the way to the ceiling.

I focused on the reading area. There was a book on

the small side table next to the chair. A bookmark hung out of the top. The title was *True Crime: Modern Forensic Tales*. Someone had handwritten the letters A and B on the cover. The bookmark was on a chapter about someone named Kenneth Barlow.

I heard a bell tinkle. I put the book back where I found it then got down on my hands and knees.

"Audrey," I crooned. "Where are you?" I didn't hear the bell again. I pushed my inner cougar forward, letting my throat and chest change enough to rumble a pleasant purr. After a few seconds, I stopped to listen. I heard the domestic cat purring. The sound came from under the dresser. "Hey, girl," I said. "You can come out." I wiggled my fingers under the raised base.

The cat purred even louder, but she didn't budge.

"Fine." I'd come back to her later. Next, I searched Abby's bedside table. There was a framed picture of her with her cat, some freesia-scented hand lotion, a box of tissues, lip balm, and nail scissors. Nothing that screamed clue.

I sighed. So far, the search was coming up empty. I took several pictures of the room with my phone, just in case, then went to the utility closet next. Inside was a small-capacity, stacked washer and dryer combo. I opened the washer. The clothes inside were damp. The dryer had clothes in it as well, a load of whites. Abby had hung scrubs on a bar over a folding table on the right side of the small space.

Next, I went into the bathroom. Once again, I was greatly disappointed. It was all standard bathroom fare. Shampoo, conditioner, body wash, face wash, toothbrush, toothpaste, mouthwash, hand soap, curling iron, and hair dryer. In the medicine cabinet, she had adhesive bandages, peroxide, isopropyl alcohol, bacitracin, and the strongest drug I could find was ibuprofen. I lifted the toilet tank lid, mostly because I'd seen someone in a movie stash stuff in there. It was empty of anything that didn't belong.

A tinkle sounded as something rubbed against my leg, making me look down. Audrey the cat, who wore a bell on her collar, had decided to come out of hiding.

"Hey, you," I said. "I bet you're hungry."

She meowed. I didn't speak domestic feline, but I took her vocalization for a yes. I reached down and scooped her up. She clung to the rubber gloves as I carried her into the living room.

"Did you find something?" Pearl said.

"A cat," I replied. "Nothing else."

"Well, crap on a cracker." Pearl sighed. "Me either. I really thought we'd find something to prove Abby didn't do this to herself."

"Oh, of that I'm certain."

"But I thought you didn't find anything."

I held up a gloved finger. "I just need to check something out." I went into the kitchen and found Audrey's food and water dishes. They were both empty. Next to her food dish was a plastic tub with cat food in it. I scooped some out and put the cat down in front of her bowl. She tucked in and immediately began eating.

"It's as I thought," I mused.

"Well, don't keep the audience in suspense," Pearl said. "Spill."

"Abby had cleaned the kitty litter, was on a second load of laundry, and hadn't left out any extra food for a cat she obviously loved very much. I think if she was going to kill herself, she wouldn't have bothered with the first two things, but she certainly would have left enough food out for Audrey just in case it took a while for someone to find her."

Which made me wonder exactly how they'd managed to find her so quickly. I'd ask Nadine to check on it.

"Is that enough to convince the police?" Pearl asked.

"Probably not. But it's enough, I think, to raise some suspicion. I'll call Nadine and Reggie tomorrow and let them know what I think." I'd promised myself I'd stop investigating deaths, and that included this one, so I added, "And then I'll let them take it from there."

"Sure," Pearl said, unconvinced.

"Can you take the cat? It can't stay here."

Pearl groaned. "Temporarily. I'm not a cat person. Or a dog person."

"Then what kind of person are you?"

"I'm a people person," she said, a sly smile quirking up her lips. "You saw a demonstration firsthand when you walked into my bathroom."

"You are too much."

"Not according to Bob."

"I don't need details."

"You'll call me tomorrow after you talk to Nadine and the doctor?"

"I promise."

"Good." She stooped down and picked up Audrey.

"Help me get her stuff to take home." She took off one glove and stroked the kitty's fur. Audrey purred. Pearl smiled.

I had a feeling Audrey would make a cat person out of Pearl yet.

CHAPTER 6

Sunday afternoon, I met Nadine and Reggie for lunch at The Cat's Meow to discuss Abby Rogers. Buzz was good enough to let Smooshie hang out in his office, and since she had a giant memory foam dog bed Buzz had bought for her and a big beef bone to chew on, she was more than happy to stay, at least for as long as it would take us to get through a meal.

Reggie hugged me and Nadine hard before we sat down. "We hardly see each other anymore," she said. "I miss you guys."

I felt a tinge of guilt. Three and a half months ago, Buzz told Nadine our secret. It took her a few days to wrap her head around the fact that her partner and her best friend were both shifters, but she ultimately came around. I wanted to tell Reggie, but it was complicated. She was in love with Parker's dad. Which means, even if she took the news as well as Nadine, she wouldn't be comfortable keeping a secret from *him*. See. Complicated. Unfortunately, it had put a strain on our together time. I'd been able to use work and classes and Parker as an excuse, but I could tell Reggie felt a shift in our dynamic.

"I miss you, too," I told her.

"How are classes going?" she asked.

"I finally finished all my general requirements and the first thirty hours of degree work. Which means," I tapped a drum roll with my fingers, "I get to start my final two semesters on Monday."

"We are going to throw the biggest party for your graduation this spring!" Nadine said. "We're so proud of you."

"Thanks," I gushed. "My schedule is pretty full. I have one class on Monday and Wednesday on campus, two on Tuesday and Thursday, one online course. It's going to be intense, between work at the rescue and my internship at Petry's Pet Clinic, but I'm really excited."

"Greer says you made the dean's list again," Reggie said. Her cheeks pinked up when she said his name.

Parker's dad, Greer, was in his early fifties, and he might have had a little gray, but it didn't make him any less handsome than his son. Like Reggie, he was part of my tribe now, my family, and I couldn't have been happier for two people to find each other. Parker's mom had died of cancer when he was in high school, and it had taken him a hot minute to adjust to his dad loving another woman. But Greer and Reggie had been seeing each other for well over a year now, and Parker had come around.

"I did make the dean's list," I bragged. I'd overcome test anxiety and had been getting the highest scores in my classes. I was proud of that accomplishment. "How are things with you and Greer?"

"Yeah," Nadine asked. "Any wedding bells in the future?" Her tone was light and teasing, but Reggie looked stricken for a moment.

"What is this, an interrogation?" She reached up and smoothed her already-smooth black hair then put her hands in her lap. I could see movement in her shoulders, as if she were fidgeting under the table.

I raised a brow. "Are you nervous about something?"

In a hushed tone, she said, "You can't tell anyone."

"Tell anyone what?" Nadine whispered.

Reggie brought her hands up to the table, her right hand covering her left. She did a slow-peek reveal to show us a beautiful circle-cut diamond set in a gold band on her left ring finger.

Nadine squealed.

Reggie's eyes widened and she slammed her right hand down over the ring. "No one can know until Greer tells Parker." She put her hands back under the table and when she brought them back up, the ring was no longer on her finger. "He's going to do it this weekend."

"This is going to be a really hard secret to keep," I said. Especially since my gut reaction to the news was to call Parker immediately and tell him everything. I would resist the urge for Reggie and Greer. "Mum's the word."

Nadine made a lock and key motion at her lips, then threw away the imaginary key. "I'm thrilled for you," she said after. "When? Where? How did it happen? We need details!"

Reggie looked around. We didn't have any diners in the booth behind us, but there were enough people in here to make the conversation not private. "I'll tell you both, I promise. Just not right now."

Freda came over to the table. "Well, hey, ladies. So good to see you. What would you all like to drink?"

"Coke," Reggie said.

"Sweet tea," I added.

"Just ice water for me," Nadine ordered.

"Coming right up." She turned on her heel and headed back behind the breakfast counter.

"Are you using a new face cream?" Reggie asked her. "Your skin looks fantastic."

"Thanks," Nadine said. She smiled. "I picked up some sea salt scrubs when Buzz and I went on vacation."

"Well, text me the name of it. I'll order me some." She pinched some loose skin on her neck. "I'm not getting any younger."

"You're stunning," I said. "Just like a blushing bride."

"Stop it." A hint of a smile crested her lips, pleased by the comparison.

"Absolutely," Nadine agreed. "You look great."

"For my age," Reggie said.

I giggled. "Because you're such a dinosaur."

Reggie squawked and flapped her hand, mimicking a pterodactyl.

Nadine snorted. "All right *Jurassic Park*, settle down."

Freda delivered our drinks. "You ready to order, or do you need a few minutes?"

"What's good today?" I asked.

"Since Buzz is back, everything. I mean, God knows the man needed a vacation, but no one works a grill like him."

Nadine said, "He's been going a little stir-crazy."

"Well, I don't know what you all did, but I haven't seen him in this good a mood in months," Freda said. "I'm glad to have the old Buzz back."

I knew why they went to California, but they'd been very buttoned up about their trip. But if he was a changed man, it's because he'd finally changed into his cougar form. Buzz had forced himself to stay human for the four months leading up to the trip to increase his chances of causing his therian DNA to go dormant long enough to get Nadine pregnant. What-ever the outcome, I was glad he was done with the nonsense. I'm not sure his or Nadine's sanity could have taken another month of his volatile mood swings.

"He's glad to be back home," Nadine said. "We both are."

Reggie ordered a chicken salad, Nadine ordered spicy chicken wings, and I ordered a triple-decker bacon cheeseburger with fried onions, and an order of sweet potato fries.

"So," Nadine said, once Freda left to put in our order, "Larry said that there was no sign of foul play at the victim's apartment." I liked that we'd had our girl time and now we were moving on to business.

"Is that so?" I asked.

"And," Reggie added, "I didn't find any defensive wounds or anything to suggest that there was some kind of fight or altercation. I don't have any blood work or tox screens back yet. Without the lab reports, I can't be sure of anything, but it looks like a fairly clear-cut case of suicide."

"Did you know Abby had a cat?" I asked them.

"I found some hairs on her," Reggie said. "So, I guess, yes. But I hadn't really thought about it."

Nadine frowned. "Larry didn't say anything about a cat."

"I don't know how they could've missed Audrey. There's a litter box in the living room, and her picture is all over the place, including a ginormous painting over her bed."

Nadine eyed me suspiciously. "How in the world do you know all this?"

I shrugged sheepishly.

"Lily," Reggie gasped. "You did not break and enter into a crime scene."

I gave them both a pointed look. "According to Larry, there was no crime. He didn't even put up any crime scene tape. Besides, it's not breaking and entering if you have the key."

Reggie scooted forward in her seat. "Where did you get a key?"

"Pearl Dixon. She and Opal used to take care of Abby's plants and cat when she was away."

Nadine stared at me. "Are your Lily-senses tingling?"

A little on the money, but okay. "The kitty litter was clean. There was a load of clothes in the washer and the dryer. And the cat's food dish was empty."

Reggie furrowed her brow. "Someone who loved their cat wouldn't leave them without food."

"Right?" I said. "If I'm going to take my life, I'm going to make sure my cat doesn't starve to death before someone finds my body."

"But she was found four hours after she died," Reggie said.

"But she couldn't have known how long it would take someone to discover her."

Nadine scoffed. "And if I was going to off myself, I wouldn't waste time doing the damn laundry."

"Exactly," I snapped.

"But that's all circumstantial." Nadine took a sip of her ice water. "There's still nothing to suggest foul play."

"Nadine's not wrong."

"But it's suspicious, right?" I asked.

"Oh, totally," they both agreed.

I lowered my voice. "She had been having an affair with a married doctor. It ended her marriage."

Nadine tapped the table. "I know her ex, Dale Rogers. I arrested him on a DUI a year ago."

"Do you know the doctor she was having the affair with?" Reggie asked.

I shook my head. "I don't."

"I'll ask Margot. She knows all the hospital gossip," Reggie said. Margot Reynolds was Reggie's office manager at her practice. "If anyone knew about the affair, she will have heard about it. I'll ask her tomorrow."

Nadine nodded. "And I'll see if Bobby will let me take another look at the apartment."

"You think he will?"

She shrugged. "He might." She gestured at Reggie. "Especially if you were to tell him your exam showed something suspicious…"

"I can't falsify an autopsy."

"But you could fudge a little in a phone call, right?" I asked.

She shook her head. "It's lying, not dessert."

Nadine grinned. "But you'll do it?"

Reggie chuckled. "I will…fudge. But I'm going to be vague as hell. If he tries to pin me down, I won't go as far as outright lying."

I nodded. "That's fair."

"Am I going to find your fingerprints all over the apartment?" Nadine asked me.

"Pearl and I wore gloves, and the only thing we took from the apartment was the cat and its necessities, food and litter box."

"Okay."

I asked a question that had been bothering me. "How did the police find her so quickly?"

"There was a noise pollution call," Nadine said. "Apparently, Abby had been playing music loudly. It's assumed that a neighbor called in the tip."

"Did anyone ever complain about Abby playing loud music before?" I asked.

"I'll find out," Nadine said.

Reggie fidgeted with her purse. "When do you go back to work?"

Nadine tugged at the ends of her hair. "Tomorrow is officially my first day back."

"If this turns into something, do you think Larry Shobe will give you the case?" I hoped he would. Nadine had more experience and smarts than Shobe.

She shrugged. "I guess we're going to find out."

"Here you go, ladies," Freda said. She expertly balanced a tray with all our food on her left forearm and served with her right hand. She set each plate down where it belonged without a hitch or wobble.

I took a big bite of the burger because I was practically starving.

Nadine laughed. "You got a little something on your chin."

I hooked the saucy juices with my finger and licked it. "I was saving it for later."

"Uh huh." She tore the meat off a wing and poked it between her lips. I watched with great interest as she basically inhaled the chicken.

"Those must be pretty tasty," Reggie observed. She forked some lettuce and grilled chicken.

"Uh huh." Nadine grunted her affirmative while devouring a second wing.

"What's going on with you?" Reggie asked Nadine.

With her mouth full, Nadine said, "Herrrfe myer-dasd garermsish."

I heard a snort of laughter from the kitchen. It made me smile. I'd missed Buzz's ease and humor. It was nice to see him back to form. Same with Nadine.

Nadine swallowed. "It's amazing what a month of sun and fun will do for your disposition."

"And appetite, apparently," I said.

"Speaking of social media," Nadine said, abruptly changing the subject. "Have you checked out Abigail Rogers' personal page for any public posts that might hint at her state of mind?"

"That's a good idea," Reggie said.

"Yeah, you should be a detective or something." I took out my phone and pulled up my social media app. Nadine and Reggie had talked me into joining, but I'd only made connections with the two of them.

"I can't believe you don't have more than two friends," Nadine scoffed.

"I have plenty of friends," I told her.

I searched the "people" tab for Abby Rogers. There were several of them, but only one had a Moonrise, Missouri, location. I clicked on Abby's profile. I honestly didn't think I would find anything illuminating, but I hoped Nadine was right, and it would give me some sense of her life.

I found several public postings by her, but they were mostly cat memes and some photos of her own cat. I searched through her pictures for anything interesting. There was one picture of a bouquet of white roses and a heart charm bracelet. The card said, "Thinking of you. XXOO." And she had commented, "Feeling loved," in the caption.

"Do you think that's the married doctor or someone else?" Reggie asked.

I set the phone down on the table so they could both see the pictures.

"No telling," Nadine replied. "Keep going, Lily."

"Oh," Reggie exclaimed when I swiped to the next photo. "There's a picture of the hospital's fundraiser from May." She pointed to a group photo that included Abby along with four men and two other women. I recognized one of the men as the doctor from the nursing home.

"Do you know who she's with?"

"The balding guy there is a Doctor Emmett Mansfield. The guy with the sandy-blond hair is Doctor Stewart Smith. The younger guy with the dark hair is Rod Simpson, a critical care nurse, the other one with graying hair and the expensive suit is the hospital administrator, Bradly Pfieffer. He asked me out once when I first moved here." She smiled at the memory. "He was a boring date, but it made me feel good to know I was still desirable after the divorce."

Reggie's ex had been a real piece of crap. He'd made her feel like all the problems in their marriage were her fault.

She continued. "I don't recognize the blonde woman. But the brunette in the red dress is Sheryl Smith. Stewart's wife. She's a doctor, too. An orthopedic surgeon." Reggie nodded. "She's probably the surgeon who took care of Opal's hip."

"Smith is married?" I asked.

"Yes," Reggie said. "But he wouldn't have an affair."

"How can you be sure?"

"I can't be a hundred percent sure, but his wife is pretty terrific. I can't see him throwing away his marriage to her for an affair."

Nadine leaned forward and tapped his face. "But who knows what motivates some men or women to cheat. Maybe she's too awesome."

Reggie nodded. "Maybe."

"What about Mansfield?" I asked.

"He's married, but I've never met his wife. I'm not sure about him." Reggie waved at the screen. "Keep going. Maybe we'll see someone else I know."

I kept scrolling, but most of Abby's posts were private, which meant casual viewers like myself couldn't see them. However, I found one paragraph she'd written on New Year's Day that said, "I resolve to value myself enough to recognize when I'm being undervalued by others." There were a bunch of thumbs-up under the post, and one heart face from Michael Lowell.

I clicked on his name and pulled up his page. He was listed as single, and like Abby, he kept most of his posts private, not public. His profile picture was, I assumed, of himself in the back of a boat on some lake, tugging on a bent fishing pole. He was a thin man with short blond hair and a pleasant face.

"Gosh, Lils. You have a bunch of notifications. Don't you ever open your social media?"

"Yes," I lied. I looked at the righthand bottom corner of the app and felt an overwhelming urge to close it out and throw my phone across the diner. It appeared I had three hundred and seventy billion notifications, probably since this was the first time I'd opened up the darn thing in a hundred months. I exaggerate, but you get the picture.

My heart skipped a beat when I saw a request to connect with Theresa Avery-Simmons from two months ago. I clicked yes and hoped that this hadn't been an olive branch that I'd accidentally ignored.

Stupid app.

I had several other connection requests from CeCe Crawford, Reggie's daughter, and four of the volunteers —Jared, Donna, Mike, and Sherry—along with Ryan Petry, Robyn Patterson, the paramedic who saved me from carbon monoxide poisoning, and Lacy Evans. That notification from Lacy was only a day old. Now, that was interesting. She'd found my personal page after seeing me at the nursing home.

I gave my pals a look of dismay. "Any of these people could call or text me just as easy. Why do they want to be my friend on the internet?"

"Because you're interesting," Reggie said.

"I work really hard to be anything *but* interesting. Interesting is overrated."

I accepted all of the requests, not because I wanted all these connections, but because I was afraid that they would see I had looked at their requests and ignored them. After I finished the last one, I noticed posts and stuff showing up on my page unbidden from all of them. Someone had a birthday, someone else was complaining about politics, another was posting vacation pictures, someone's aunt died, another lost their pet of eighteen years, and there was a great temptation to click the thumbs-up on each of them.

Instead, I closed out the app and pushed my phone away.

Nadine grabbed it.

"What are you doing?" I tried to take it from her, but she held it out of reach.

"I'm just adding one more friend." She typed in Michael Lowell's name and clicked the request button.

"He doesn't know me from hayseed. He's not going to accept."

Nadine's eyebrows raised as she handed me back my phone. "He already did. Now we can see if Lowell is a suspect or a potential witness."

"Is there room at this table for one more?"

"Sure, Pearl." Reggie scooted toward the window side of the bench seat. "You're more than welcome."

"How'd you get into town?" I asked when she sat down. Pearl had changed her hair color to a vibrant indigo, giving a whole new meaning to blue-haired old lady.

She flattened her lips and gave me a meaningful stare, before replying, "A friend drove me." She emphasized "friend."

"Oh." Bob Tolliver. "Is your, uhm, friend coming in?"

"I told my, uhm, friend that I would be getting a ride home with you," Pearl said with a lot of sarcasm for a seventy-something-year-old. "So, I sent my, uhm, friend away."

"Is friend code for booty call?" Nadine asked, punctuating the words with a ravaged chicken wing bone.

I widened my eyes at the daggers Pearl shot in my direction. "Big mouth."

I shook my head. "I haven't said a word."

Reggie coughed.

"Oh my gosh!" Nadine clapped. "I'm right?"

"Why don't we spend a little less time investigating my personal business and spend a little more time figuring out who killed Abby?"

"I'm sorry, Pearl," Nadine said. "My bad."

I felt the familiar vibration of a lie. Nadine wasn't sorry at all.

Freda came over to the table. "What can I get you, Pearl?"

"Me, nothing. But these three will take the check."

"We will? Are we leaving?"

"Abby's mother is going to be visiting Opal in about half an hour. She'd like you to be there. Something about how you always know when someone is lying or telling the truth."

"Just a keen intuition," I said.

"Whatever." Pearl stood up. "Point is, we have to go."

"Can we come?" Nadine asked.

"I don't think there's room in Lily's truck for all of us."

"We can take my sedan," Reggie said.

"Fine. You two can come," Pearl agreed.

The frantic patter of nails along the linoleum tile forced me to jump up and put myself between the elderly Pearl and my seventy-five-pound bundle of energy.

Buzz stood in the archway. "Sorry, Lils. She got away from me."

"She's fast like that."

"I call shotgun," Pearl said. "Deputy Nosy-Parker and Lily can sit in the back with the fur ball."

CHAPTER 7

"Oh my lord," Nadine croaked. She jammed her finger on the window button to no avail. "Damn it, Reggie. Unlock the windows or roll them down."

"What are you all going on about?" Pearl asked.

The smell must have crept to the front of the sedan, because Reggie groaned and hit all the window buttons at once. I held on to Smooshie's collar so she wouldn't get any ideas about escaping her own gas bomb.

"It's toxic," Reggie said. "What have you been feeding her?" She drove with one hand on the wheel, the other waving in front of her face, and the strong breeze coming into the windows had started to undo her updo.

"I can't smell a thing." Pearl touched her nose and smiled. "Old showgirl accident."

Smooshie, the smelly offender, wiggled and squirmed across my lap, her tail lethally smacking Nadine across the shoulder. I was holding on, laughing and gagging at the same time. She licked my nose. "Smoosh!"

"Make it stop," Nadine said. "Please make it stop."

Smooshie whined. "Uh oh." I knew that whine. My girl had to go number two, and she was almost at the point of no return. "We better pull over."

"Is someone going to puke?" Pearl asked. "I have a strong stomach except when I see puke."

"Someone is going to poop!" I said with more urgency.

Reggie pointed ahead. "We're a block from the nursing home."

Nadine hung her head out the window. "Pull over the car!"

"All right," Reggie said. "Just hold your horse, and by horse, I mean dog."

The car slowed, Smooshie's whining increased. She tried to circle between Nadine and me. "Hang on, girl. Almost free." I undid my seat belt, ready to jump out with her when Reggie parked. "Hurry!"

The car stopped and Reggie threw it in park. "Go, go, go!"

I shoved the door open, and Smooshie jumped over my lap onto the sidewalk. I held on to her leash, grabbed my purse and piled out after her, thankful for the handful of dog waste bags I'd thrown in there before I'd left Parker's today. Her eight-foot-long rope leash gave her enough room to get to the grass without me. She had already circled once then squatted as I closed the car door behind me.

We were close enough to walk to the nursing home.

"Go ahead," I told the ladies. "I'll meet you all at the manor."

None of them argued with me.

After Smooshie had finished her important business, I bagged the evidence. "Well, girl, let's see if we can find a trash can around here." Smooshie barked and did a half jump, more from relief, I was certain, than finding an appropriate place to dispose of the bag. I wrapped the rope leash around her chest and pulled the end through the extra ring to make it into a harness.

The Moonrise Manor was H shaped, which I learned the hard way by walking the perimeter of the place in search of a dumpster or a covered bin. The first nook of the H was fenced off. The interior was graveled with an outbuilding, a lean-to with a riding mower and a push mower underneath, but no trash cans. Not that it would have done me any good, since I had no plans to hop the six-foot chain-link. I kept going around, occasionally glancing into a window to see a resident watching television or sleeping.

I rounded the corner of the long backside of the building and the second nook opened up into a court-yard-style area. Smooshie's ears twitched with excitement as we passed through a white picket gate. The temperature was seventy degrees, which to me was perfect, but both the elderly women enjoying the fresh air were wearing sweaters and long pants. I recognized one of the ladies as Jane Davidson. She was sleeping in her wheelchair, her head down.

I looped Smooshie's leash over one of the fence's concrete posts and approached her. Her lower jaw almost looked unhinged and dry spittle had created what looked like a white powder in the corner of her mouth.

"Mrs. Davidson?" I said. When she didn't wake up, I placed my hand on her shoulder and gave it a mild shake. "Ma'am?"

Her skin had a waxy, almost yellow appearance. I touched her wrist. Cold, clammy, and she had a weak pulse.

The woman sitting on the bench said, "She's been asleep since I got out here. She's really tired."

"How long ago was that?"

"Honestly, I don't know. I've been out here since just a bit after lunch, and I finish eating around one."

It was one thirty-five now. I rubbed my knuckles against her chest to see if I could rouse a response. Mrs. Davidson barely stirred. Her body carried a strange odor, one that I couldn't quite put my finger on. I tapped into my werecougar, allowing her to take over my senses. There was a sharp odor that smelled vaguely of medicine, but more like mouthwash without the mint added.

I knew Mrs. Davidson was diabetic. From everything I'd read, if she were experiencing a high blood sugar, she would smell fruity, as if she'd been drinking alcohol. But this was more stringent without any sweetness. "I think her blood sugar is low," I said.

The woman next to her gave me a *what do you want me to do about it?* look.

"Hang in there, Jane. I'll be right back." I set the waste bag next to the bench then glanced over at

Smooshie, who was happily eating a tuft of grass that I was sure I'd be cleaning out of the carpet at home later. "You're not a cow," I said to her. "Stop grazing."

I walked quickly to the door, opened it, and stuck my head in. The short hall was empty, along with the two nurses' stations on either side.

I could hear the beep of call lights. "Hello," I yelled. "We need some help. Hello? Help!"

"Help!" I heard an elderly gentleman shout. Then a woman several rooms down joined in.

Great. I was starting a riot.

I glanced back at Mrs. Davidson. I didn't want to have to leave her or Smooshie, so I tried again, even louder. "I need some help in the courtyard!"

Lacy Evans, her face flushed and her expression concerned, came up the hallway pushing her cart at a fast walk. "What's happening, Lily?"

"Mrs. Davidson. She's unconscious. I think she might be having a hypoglycemic attack."

Now Lacy looked irritated. "She's probably just sleeping. A lot of these people are hard sleepers." As she said this, she was pulling out a small machine from her cart and some kind of pen that she loaded with a tiny needle.

"I hope that's all it is," I said. "But she's super unresponsive, her pulse is weak, and her skin feels cold and damp."

She poked a small tab into one end of the machine. "A glucose monitor," she explained. "Lead the way."

"She's just outside here." I opened the door wide, and Lacy brushed past me.

She knelt down next to Mrs. Davidson and took her hand. She clicked the pen against a finger, and that's when I observed that most of her fingertips were purple and bruised from daily monitoring. She tapped the tiny droplet of blood against the tab sticking out of the machine, then set it down on the bench. She pressed her index and middle finger to the inner part of Mrs. Davidson's wrist.

"Her pulse is faint." She pulled a stethoscope from her pocket, put it in her ears and pressed the drum to Mrs. Davidson's chest. "Damn it. Her heartbeat is going a mile a minute." The machine beeped. "Her blood sugar is at nineteen! How in the world could that happen? It was two hundred and eighty before lunch. I told the nurse, and he gave her some regular insulin like it was ordered, but it shouldn't have dropped it this low."

She jumped up and ran inside, a few seconds later reemerging with a red box. She opened it and took out a prefilled syringe, removed the safety cap off the large-bore needle, then grabbed a vial that was inside the box. She popped off the red cap, stuck the needle in, depressed all the liquid into the vial. Keeping the needle in place, she shook the vial until whatever was in there was mixed with the contents of the syringe, then turned it up and pulled it all back into the barrel of the syringe.

"Glucagon," Lacy explained as she withdrew the needle and put the whole thing back into its box. "It will raise her blood sugar." To Mrs. Davidson, she said,

"Stay with me, Jane." She gestured to me. "Help me lean her to the left."

I did, holding Mrs. Davidson off to one side, while Lacy lowered her pants down to expose her hip. She pinched up the skin and stuck Mrs. Davidson with a quickness that would make a shifter proud, then she pushed the plunger all the way down in a slow, steady measure.

I helped Mrs. Davidson up. "Now what?"

"It takes about ten minutes for this stuff to work," Lacy said. "I'm going to get a nurse and call an ambulance. Can you stay with her until I get back?"

"I'm not going anywhere," I told her. "And hey, you were pretty incredible just now. You're going to make a great nurse."

Lacy nodded, her eyes starting to tear up. "Thanks."

"Your dog is going nuts over there," the old woman said.

I looked at Smooshie, who was now on her back and wiggling side to side, a recent habit she'd picked up. Parker theorized that it was ancient pack instinct kicking in since she ran with a cougar every week, but I'd given her enough baths to know she just liked to roll around in wild animal poop.

"Yep," I said, as I waited for Lacy's return. "That's my girl. Nuts."

Mrs. Davidson muttered something. Good. The injection Lacy gave her was working. When the nurse, a guy named Rick, showed up with Lacy and began checking out Mrs. Davidson, I took the opportunity to check on Smooshie, who was now pacing back and forth again.

I took her outside the gate and let her lead me several yards away from the courtyard. She circled, sniffed, then circled again, then sniffed. Then sniffed some more. Her tail wagged as whatever scent she'd caught distracted her from the fact that she needed to poop again.

"Come on, girl." I wanted to get back and see how Mrs. Davidson was doing.

Lacy had been so calm in her quick assessment and treatment of the elderly woman. She certainly wasn't the young girl who'd crashed her car my first week in Moonrise. She'd left her infant at home by himself while she'd run out to the convenience store for a fountain drink, and nearly ran a pedestrian over in the process. She'd been wearing pajamas and house slippers, and she had asked me to call her mom to pick up her son. I had debated on whether calling child services wouldn't have been a better solution, but her mom worked for my uncle, and I'd decided to let family take care of family. After all, I'd had my share of tough times as a teenager trying to take care of a kid.

The way she'd handled this crisis, and the fact that she was going to school and getting her life in order, made me glad I hadn't put more roadblocks in her way.

I focused my hearing toward the courtyard and heard the nurse tell Lacy that the blood sugar was fifty now, so on its way up. "Good job," he'd told her. "How in the world did her blood sugar drop like that?"

Lacy replied, "I don't know. She's had lunch since

her insulin injection. I double checked the dose. She shouldn't have crashed like that."

Paula the social worker and Annie the activity director hustled out into the courtyard. "The ambulance is here. How did this happen?"

"Honestly, I don't know," Rick said. "She got her normal injection before lunch. Maybe she didn't eat? Even so, it's a pretty extreme drop."

Paula tugged at the hem on her shirt. "This is not good."

"I'll ask the aides if she ate her lunch," Annie said.

"And how did she get outside?" Paula asked. "Who brought her out here?"

"I'll find out," Rick said. Then the paramedics came through and, within a short time, they had Jane up on a stretcher. After they hooked her up to a few things, they strapped her down and the group of them went back inside the facility.

Smoosh pulled on the leash and pawed at whatever wonderful treasure she'd found. "What in the world has you so fascinated?"

I bent over for a closer look. Something red was sticking to a grass clump. I picked it up. It was a crumpled square of cellophane. It had a citrus scent. "You find the weirdest things," I told Smooshie as I placed the trash into an empty poop bag. "Are you going to go or what?"

She eyeballed me, staring at the bag where I'd hidden her treasure, and twitched her ears back and forth expectedly.

I laughed. "You want a treat for your find?"

She barked excitedly at the word "treat." I took a small pouch of training treats from my purse. "Sit then."

Smooshie sat, but her helicopter tail was swishing so hard I doubted her butt touched the ground. She laid her ears back, her chin up, making her look very much like a seal. "Who could resist that face?" I asked when I presented her with the dime-sized delicacy. "Easy now."

She took the treat gently, like the good girl she is, then inhaled it as if it were a dying man's last meal.

"Lily," I heard Nadine call.

Reggie, Pearl, Opal, and Nadine were in the courtyard. Opal was sitting on the bench, a walker pushed out in front of her. I hoped I hadn't missed the chance to talk with Abby's mom.

"I'll be right there," I said, loud enough for them to hear. Smooshie, who'd apparently lost the urge to poop, led me in their direction.

CHAPTER 8

The elderly woman who had been out there with Mrs. Davidson was still on her bench, enjoying the afternoon as if her neighbor hadn't almost died. I'd seen that kind of ambivalence in certain sects of the shifter populations who barely batted an eyelash at extreme violence.

"How'd you end up back here?" Nadine asked me. Smooshie rubbed her shoulder against Nadine's leg and got a scritch behind the ears as a reward.

"I was looking for—"

"No, no, no," Reggie said, cutting me off. "What the ever-loving…" She was lifting her patent-leather, kitten-heeled pump from the ground, Smooshie's poop bag clinging to the one-inch spike. "Why? Why would someone put this here?"

Nadine raised a brow at me.

"As I was saying, I was trying to find a trash can," I said in my defense. "But there isn't a single one outside this entire building."

"Which answers my question," Nadine said. "About how you got back here."

Reggie scowled as she delicately extracted the biodegradable bag from her shoe. "This is so gross."

"It'll wash," I told her. Nadine snickered.

Reggie stuck her tongue out at the both of us. "I don't think I like either of you very much."

"I'll buy you lunch this week," I told her. I dug around in my purse for a tissue and found a fast food napkin. "Here."

She wiped the poop off the end of her heel and held the soiled napkin away from her as she looked around. "Trash?"

"My point exactly," I said.

Opal, who'd been silently watching us, let out a big belly guffaw that ended in a wheeze of chuckles. "Oh, God," she said. "I needed you all today."

"Where's Abby's mom?" I asked, reining in Smooshie when she made a nosedive for Pearl's crotch.

"Dang it, Lily!" Pearl swatted at the air where Smooshie's nose had been and stumbled back. I was grateful she remained upright.

I grimaced. "Sorry."

Opal laughed harder. Pearl, at hearing her sister's reprieve from her grief, shook her head and smiled. "I'll survive."

Nadine answered my question about Abby's mom. "Melinda is up in the office talking to Ruby Davis, the administrator, and Dawn Welch, the director of nursing. She said she'd meet us out here."

"How'd you all know I was in the courtyard?"

RENEE GEORGE

"This place isn't that big," Nadine said. "We would have had to have been deaf not to hear. We would have been down here quicker but…"

"I'm slow these days," Opal supplied. "Besides, at first we thought it might be old Gerald Greenspan. He hollers for help all the time then gets a few others going as well."

"Well, I'm glad you're here. I didn't even think about what I'd do with Smooshie once we got here."

A middle-aged woman, maybe in her early fifties, walked into the courtyard. Her hair was professionally colored a honey blonde with delicate strands of high and low lights. She glanced around at all of us, her tired gaze finally landing on Opal.

"What will we do now?" the woman asked, her eyes filling with tears.

The rawness of her words made me recoil. Maybe talking to Abby's mother two days after her daughter's death had been a really bad idea.

"I'm so sorry for your loss," I told her, because there was nothing else to say, nothing that could help, anyhow.

"Melinda, this is Lily Mason," Opal said. She held out her hand, and the woman sat down on the bench next to her.

"Did you know my Abby?" Melinda asked.

"I met her recently. She was easy to like."

Melinda smiled. "She always had a way of drawing people to her."

Smooshie, thankfully, showed little interest in Abby's mom and had flopped down by my feet with a loud huff, giving up on any more exploration. "I could see that about her." She had been funny and charming, and the fact that Opal had loved her was enough for me.

"Melinda, Lily has promised to find out what happened to Abby. She's going to get justice for our girl," Opal said.

Oh, Goddess me. "Now, Opal, I can't promise all that."

Melinda looked up at me with wet, pleading eyes. "I've read the newspaper article where you were instrumental in capturing the dentist and his wife who killed that poor preacher's wife."

Reverend, I mentally corrected. Katherine Kapersky had been the wife of Reverend Kapersky. The reverend had been a decent man. He left the church after Tom Jones' conviction and moved away from Moonrise. Presumably for a fresh start. I hoped he'd found some peace. His wife had not been a saint, but she hadn't deserved death.

"I agreed to look into it, Opal. I can't make any assurances about what I'll find."

"But you're already convinced she didn't kill herself," she said. "The cat. Audrey. Pearl told me about her not having any food and what you said about it."

I glared at Pearl. She patted her blue hair and avoided eye contact. "I didn't know it was a secret."

"It isn't a secret, but it also isn't concrete evidence of foul play."

Nadine nodded. "Lily's right."

"What about you, Doctor Crawford?" Melinda

asked. "Have you found anything to explain my Abby's death?"

Reggie frowned. "I don't have any real answers, yet. I can tell you that I haven't found any evidence of trauma." Her voice softened; her gaze full of compassion. "I think she died peacefully, if that's any comfort."

"I wish it was," Melinda said. "I just can't stand the idea of people thinking my daughter would do this. And why? Abby had so much to live for. She had no reason to take her own life."

I could feel a tingle of a lie. Melinda was holding back about her daughter. If anyone understood secrets and the need for them, it was me. However, now was not the time. Not if we were going to get to the truth of the matter.

I put my hand on Melinda's shoulder and pushed my will, not hard, just a nudge to see if she would open up. My power couldn't compel someone to spill their guts if they really didn't want anyone to know. I had a feeling Melinda wanted to tell us, but she was afraid. Of what? Probably that we might judge her daughter, or maybe her.

"It's hard losing someone we love, but death can't undo their life. There's always good with the bad and bad with the good." My brother Danny had been funny and charming and likeable, but he'd also been troubled, ran with a rough crowd, and had gotten into hard drugs. It didn't mean I loved him less, but the truth of his life had tainted the police investigation into his death. "Whatever you tell us, I promise, it won't stop me from finding out the truth of Abby's death. Can you think of anything that might have pushed Abby too far? To a breaking point?"

A sob forced its way from Melinda's throat. She took several deep breaths, then said, "Abby was taking antidepressants. It's my fault." She covered her face with her hands. "It's all my fault."

"How?" Nadine asked.

"She struggled after her divorce. Dale, her ex, he pretty much had blackmailed Abby into giving him the house and not going after him for alimony. She'd lost so much of her spark and I worried..." Her voice trailed off.

"You worried she might do something terrible to herself." I lifted my hand from her shoulder. I shook my head. I didn't believe Abby had been depressed, not anymore. Depressed people didn't care about things like laundry and kitty litter. And the Abby I had met had been full of energy and happiness. "Please don't blame yourself. I think you did what a mother is supposed to do. You helped your daughter through a terrible time and got her to the other side."

The tension lines around Melinda's eyes eased as she met my gaze. "Thank you."

"Do you know if Abby was seeing someone?" I hated asking this next question, but as her mom, she might know. "A married someone?"

Melinda's mouth pursed and her eyes narrowed. "She hadn't been seeing him. Not for a while now." She shook her head. "And before you ask, I don't know who he was. She wouldn't tell me. But she did promise me it was over. She'd had a few dates with other men the last three months. So, I believed her when she said it."

"Anyone she was getting serious about?"

Melinda shook her head again. "She said one guy was texting her a lot, but she wasn't interested in seeing him more."

Phone records. That would be a job for Nadine.

I nodded. "Is there anything else you can think of that might offer some insight?"

As if she had an a-ha moment, Melinda's eyes widened. "I think she was having trouble with someone here at the nursing home. She complained one night about something not being right, but when I pressed her, she said she couldn't talk about it. I just assumed it was normal work drama. It's probably nothing, but…I don't know."

"I'll look into it," I said. I smiled sympathetically. "Thank you for talking to us, Melinda. I know it can't be easy."

"Abby trusted Opal. Opal trusts you." She said it like it was an absolute.

The woman who'd been sitting across the way had been quiet the whole time we'd been talking. She raised up to her feet and said, "I really liked Abby. She was a good one."

I'd completely forgotten about her. I remembered Pearl saying how she was over seventy, so invisible was easy, and I flushed with guilt. "Can we help you get back to your room?"

"I'm old, sweetie, but I can still move these old bones."

She dusted her blue polyester pants at the butt. "That was fast work with Jane. She usually naps out here after lunch, so I wouldn't have thought a thing about her." She walked toward the door. "Name's Mabel. Stop in and see me next time you're here. I'm always around somewhere."

Melinda stood up. "I better get going." She addressed Reggie. "Do you know when I can have the funeral home pick up Abby?" Her eyes watered with tears again.

"I'll call you as soon as I know. It shouldn't be more than a day or two," Reggie offered.

"We better get going, too," Nadine said. She looked at the time on her phone.

"Do you have to be somewhere?"

She gave me a pointed stare. "As a matter of fact, I do." She knew about my lie detector abilities, and the look warned me not to test her.

I gave a little toss up of my hands. "Okay, you don't have to tell me." I knew she would eventually tell me what was going on with her when she was ready. Now probably wasn't the best time."

Smooshie, who must have felt it was time to go, stood up, her tail whacking between my leg and Reggie's.

Reggie smiled down at her. "It's a good thing you're cute."

Smooshie pressed her nose into Reggie's hand for a quick pet, for which Reggie obliged, laughing when Smooshie licked her palm. My girl could charm a unicorn out of her horn.

"I'm going to stay with Opal," Pearl said. "You girls go ahead."

"Are you sure?" I asked. "Won't you need a ride home?"

"I'll find my own ride."

I raised my brow. "I'm sure you will."

The conversation with Abby's mom had given me more questions than answers. Was she still on antidepressants? Was she still seeing the married doctor? Or was she being stalked by a new guy? And what about her ex-husband? The ex always seemed like a good place to start in a case like this. Also, she was having trouble at work. With whom? Why? And was the drama enough trouble that someone would want her out of the way?

CHAPTER 9

R eggie dropped Nadine and me back at the diner. We all said our goodbyes before Smooshie and I headed to Parker's place. I'd called him to let him know we were on the way, but still, I was surprised when I saw him waiting in his driveway for me, Elvis already in his truck.

I rolled down the window. "What's up?"

He walked up to the driver's side and leaned in. "Dad called. His truck broke down just out past your place at the Winslows."

"A mechanic with a mechanical problem, huh? That's ironic." Greer owned The Rusty Wrench and, as it happened, had been the first person in town that I met after my truck sputtered to a halt in his parking lot. "Doesn't he have tools on him?"

He shrugged. "Yeah, but not the right part. I'm going to swing by his shop before I head out."

"Do you want me to go with you to get him?"

Parker smiled. "Nah." He dipped his head inside

the cab and kissed me. "You go on home. You and Smooshie have a good run, and I'll swing by after I get Dad sorted."

"All right," I said. "I'll see you after a while."

"Crocodile," Parker finished. He reached over and tapped my nose with his finger.

"You booped me," I said.

He laughed and patted the window ledge. "I'll follow you out." As he went to his truck, he had an extra spring in his step that on several levels concerned me. Parker was the one person, as my mate, who didn't set off my tingles when he lied. But his oddly good mood and the nose boop made me wonder what in the world he was up to.

My suspicion kicked up several notches when Parker didn't stop into his dad's garage. He followed me out of town and down the rural gravel road I lived on. I couldn't stop glancing back at him in the rearview mirror. He was smiling and talking to Elvis the whole time.

When I got close to my driveway, I could see several vehicles up near the house and the trailer. "What's happening?" I asked Smooshie, so she shoved her head out the top of the partially opened passenger window and sniffed.

"That's no answer," I told her as I turned in. Parker turned in after me.

I recognized Greer's truck, the one that had supposedly broken down. Why was he at my place? Ryan Petry's fancy sports car was over by the trailer. There was another car that surprised me. It belonged to

Theresa Simmons.

Why was everyone at my place? I actually felt a little panicked as I got out of the truck.

Then I saw them. Two large pallets loaded with rectangular boxes.

My mood instantly brightened. "My floors have arrived!" Smooshie bailed out of the truck after me. "We have floors, Smoosh!" I said, scratching her neck.

Parker, who'd parked right behind me, grinned as he and Elvis piled out of his truck. "Let's go take a look at them."

"Surprise!" came a chorus of voices from inside the house as my friends poured out onto the porch. Greer, Reggie, Nadine, Buzz, Theresa, Keith, Ryan and, surprisingly, Paul Simmons. He and Ryan were seeing each other, but as far as I knew, it was still on the hush-hush. Mostly, anyhow.

"What are you all doing here?" I asked.

"What does it look like?" Ryan said. "We're having a floor-laying party?"

Parker slid a box from the top and popped it open. "Come take a look at your new floors."

The laminated tiles mimicked weathered hickory, almost gray color, like old barn wood. My chest squeezed with joy.

"I love them." The floors were the last thing I needed to get done before I could finally move out of the trailer and into the house.

Paul, who was the manager of Hayes Home Improvement Center, had given me a sweetheart deal on the tiles, since the manufacturer was no longer making this particular pattern, and a month earlier he'd found several remnants at a great price that I used for the upstairs bedrooms. The only big expense had been the underlayment, but Parker had helped me put that down last weekend.

"How did you all arrange this? I mean to be here, right when the floors came?"

"For a smart girl…" Nadine said. She looked over at Paul. "He told Ryan, and Ryan told us, and we all agreed that it was time you got to live in this house of yours. You shouldn't have to spend one more night in that tin can." She pointed at the trailer.

"It's not that bad." Besides, these days I'd spent as much time in Parker's bed as my own. But still, I was excited about the prospect of having a real home of my own. To both Reggie and Nadine, I asked, "How did you guys beat me over here?" Reggie was wearing jeans and a plain blue T-shirt. "And when did you find the time to change clothes?"

"I had this in my car," she said. "And we basically raced over." Both my best friends laughed.

I glanced at Greer. I knew about the engagement, and I could tell by the look on his face that Reggie had let him know that I knew. His brow furrowed, but I smiled and gave him a nod. His secret was safe with me. For now. The tension in his forehead eased.

I gave all of my friends a once-over. "You all can't want to spend your day off messing with my house," I said.

"We certainly can," Buzz replied for the group. He traipsed down the steps and put his arm around my shoulder. "I can't think of a better way to spend a Sunday. How about you guys?"

A lot of nods and mutters of agreement went around.

I met Theresa's gaze. "It's so nice to have you here."

"Of course." She glanced away and back, as if shy. "I wanted to help."

"Don't overdo it," Parker warned her. "Don't want you going into labor."

Keith chuckled. "I've put her on strict water duty. She's not allowed to lift anything heavier than a gallon of milk."

Theresa patted her stomach. "Do you hear that, baby? Your dad is already telling me how to do my job."

I grinned. "You're going to be a great mom."

She smiled and didn't look away this time when her gaze met mine. "Thank you, Lily."

"And," Buzz said dramatically as he pointed to some red coolers near the porch I hadn't noticed. "I brought burgers and dogs to burn on the grill and all the fixings that go with them."

Ryan grinned and ran a hand through his thick, perfect hair. He pointed out a large blue cooler near his car. "And I brought beer."

"It's perfect." My heart thumped in my chest until I thought it would burst through my rib cage.

Buzz still had his arm around my shoulders. "This is all because of you, kiddo. I never thought I could have this kind of life, you know, where I could have a real home. Family. But you make me feel like it's really possible."

"It is," I said. I prayed I was right, because all these people were my family now. Cougars in the wild tended to be solitary creatures, preferring to be on their own, but that wasn't how I wanted to live my life. I'd been alone long enough in Paradise Falls.

Buzz walked back over to Nadine, and they began to move the boxes of flooring into the house with the others.

Parker came up behind me. "Surprise," he said softly.

"I knew you were up to something," I said.

He wrapped his arms around my waist, his hands settling on my belly. He kissed my neck. "I thought your mojo didn't work on me."

"It doesn't. You're just a really bad liar." I turned in his arms and slid my palms up his chest and crossed them behind his neck. "So, you agree with Buzz," I said quietly. "You couldn't think of any better way to spend a Sunday?"

"If that's on the table," he replied, his smile sly.

"How about after we get the floor laid first?" I told him.

"Then I get laid," he said.

I giggled because I couldn't help myself. "If you're not too worn out."

"Challenge accepted," he said, rewarding me with a kiss full of heat and promise. "We best get started."

"Uh huh," I agreed a little breathlessly.

"You two either get a room or grab some boxes," Buzz said.

I blushed as it dawned on me that, with his shifter hearing, he had probably heard every part of our flirty conversation. Living in a human town was dulling my wits. I'd have never been that indiscreet back in Paradise Falls.

As a group, we hauled about thirty boxes of tiles inside the dining room, since it would be the last room to get a new floor, before the group stopped to take a breather.

Thanks to my second nature, I was stronger than most human women and men, but Parker could definitely carry his own weight. He leaned against the arch leading into the living room, watching me as I ripped into the open box.

"You're kind of amazing," he said. "Just in case I haven't told you lately."

"Just kind of?"

"Maybe a little more than that."

We let Paul take the lead as the expert, since he talked to people all day about this kind of DIY home improvement. Before long, the afternoon dragged into the evening, and by the time it was dark around seven o'clock, we'd finished all the living room, the hallway, and the kitchen. Buzz went to cook, while the rest of us grabbed beers and started on clean-up duty. By the time we were done, the burgers and hot dogs were ready to be consumed.

Luckily, Greer had the foresight to bring lawn chairs, and while there wasn't enough for everyone, between the porch steps, my kitchen chairs, and the lawn chairs, we all had a place to sit.

"All we're missing is a campfire," Ryan said.

Paul nudged his shoulder. "You want some marshmallows to roast as well?" He laughed.

"I'd love some marshmallows," I said, then took a big bite of my juicy burger. After putting in several long hours of hard work, and with my metabolism, I worried I would need a dozen to replace the calories I'd burned. Smooshie put her head on my knee and I pinched her off a generous portion. She wolfed it down, then put her head on my knee for another bite.

"You are spoiling her rotten," Buzz said. He held two plates, both with big patties, medium rare. He handed one to Parker and one to me. "I didn't put any seasoning on these for Elvis and Smoosh."

"Ah, lookie," I told my girl. "Uncle Buzz wuvs you."

"Har har," Buzz replied. He finished serving everyone else before bringing his own plate to the circle and taking the seat on the other side of Nadine. "So, Nadine tells me you're looking into the Rogers girl's death."

I had just taken another bite of burger, so I nodded and grunted, "Uh huh."

"Freda said Lacy lives on the second floor of the same apartment complex. You might want to talk to her about some of the comings and goings from Abby's place."

I finished chewing and swallowing. "You're not going to tell me to keep my nose out of it?"

"Would it do me any good?"

Nadine snorted.

"No," I said honestly.

"That's what I thought. Besides, I liked Abby. She came in sometimes to have lunch with Opal and Pearl. They've both been good customers and good friends to me over the years. If Opal is asking, then I can't tell you no."

I nodded. "I care about them, too."

"I can't believe the darn fool woman broke her hip," Greer said.

"Actually, it was her femur, the long bone in her leg."

"Those flamingos are a freaking maze," Nadine said. "I got called out there one night because Pearl had heard something or someone out in the bushes, and I almost broke my neck tripping over one."

Theresa, who'd just come back from the trailer after her umpteenth bathroom break, said, "Did I hear you guys talking about Abby Rogers?"

"Yes." I watched Keith get up when she arrived and help her down into her chair. The way he doted on her was sweet and nothing less than she deserved after years of putting up with an abusive husband. "Did you know her?"

"I did. Her ex and my ex used to run in the same circles." I could hear the bitter in her tone as she thought about Jock Simmons. He'd been murdered because he was an awful human being. I'd actually felt sorry for the girl who'd killed him.

Theresa continued. "Abby and I ended up at the wives' table more than once at several dinner parties. I had a feeling we were kindred spirits, if you catch my meaning."

Jock used to hit Theresa. I'd seen the bruises for myself more than once. "Do you think he beat her?"

"No." She shook her head. "But I do think he was abusive. And I think he cheated. Do you think Dale had anything to do with her death?"

"I know Dale," Ryan said. "He teaches part-time at the college. He's got issues, but I don't think he's a killer."

"Well, sure," I said. "If he abuses women, he definitely has issues. But I've seen plenty of people without so-called issues kill, so I don't see why it couldn't have been him."

All eyes were on me now. I gulped, remembering that only two other people in the group knew Buzz and I were shifters.

I amended my statement. "You know, on those reality crime shows. It's not like I know a bunch of murderers in real life."

There were a few uncomfortable chuckles, but happily the conversation moved on.

"I just meant that Dale is, well, he's a jerk, but I don't see it. He was angry about the infidelity, but I do think he loved her as much as someone like him can," Ryan explained.

"Like him?"

"He has a chip on his shoulder. Poor kid made good. A bad childhood can really mess up some adults." Ryan sighed. "I shouldn't be sharing this, but he's been in counseling. I think he's really trying to fix the way he sees the world."

Reggie, the voice of reason, said, "No amount of speculation is going to do us any good until I find out the cause of death. She could very well have taken her own life."

"Sure," Nadine said. "Play devil's advocate, if you will. But I trust Lily's gut if she thinks something's off about this."

"My gut is not saying a whole lot right now." It growled. Loudly. Everyone laughed. "Okay. It's saying it's time for another burger."

When everyone was leaving, Buzz gave me a hug and said, "Talk to Lacy. Freda didn't say much, but I got the distinct impression that Lacy knows something. Something that she won't volunteer without a little prompting."

"Thanks," I said. Then, "Hey, when are you and Nadine going to tell me about your trip?"

He kissed my cheek. "Soon. I promise."

After everyone left, Parker and I went into the house and sat down on the floor against the wall near the fireplace to admire all of our handiwork. Elvis and Smooshie followed us in, both sniffing around the new floors, I imagined, taking in all the different scents of the worker bees.

I sighed contentedly. The place finally looked like a real home.

"It's beautiful." Happiness welled up inside me and spilled out as tears of joy. "I can't believe you all did this for me."

"Don't you know, Lily Mason, that I would do just about anything for you?"

"I do know." I turned into him and lay across his lap.

He cradled me in his arms. "I love you. We all do."

"I do want to live with you, Parker. I hope you know that I do. I just don't want to leave this place. I love this property, and now I love my house. I can't live in town. I'm just not made for neighbors."

"Then how about Elvis and I move out here with you?"

"You'd do that? Give up your place?"

Parker laughed. "I talked to a realtor last week. There's a dog and cat groomer couple looking for a place to live and open a full-time business. The house and the old shelter can give them exactly what they need."

"Have they made an offer?"

"Yes, but I told them I had to talk to someone about it first." He kissed me and sizzle zipped through me. "So, I'm talking. What say you, Lils? Want a roommate?"

"No," I told him. "I want a mate."

"Is that a yes?" He looked hopeful.

"It's a yes."

He kissed me again. This time the sizzle went right to my toes. His fingers wound through my hair. "The floors have been laid," he said.

"Well," I said. "A deal's a deal."

CHAPTER 10

The next morning, Parker took Elvis and Smooshie with him to the shelter so I could prepare for my early class, Veterinarian Diagnostic Imaging. The course description described the class as an in-depth study into the history and practice of veterinarian medical radiology. I would be learning the history of radiology, along with how to take the x-rays and develop them.

I'd seen Kelly, at vet tech at Ryan's practice, perform several radiological images on dogs and cats brought into the office. The clinic had an up-to-date digital imaging table with a mobile arm and an adjustable seventeen-inch square flat panel that displayed an image immediately on the monitor. It required a fraction of the time the old tables that used film cassettes used to take, so most of the animals that needed x-rays these days didn't need sedation unless they were in a lot of pain or couldn't hold still for a few seconds.

I didn't do much except observe, but I thought it was fascinating. I hoped the class would teach us a little about the diagnostic aspect of radiology as well. It wouldn't be in my job description, but I was still very curious.

Dr. Milo Cramer, a retired veterinarian radiologist by practice, taught the course. I'd met him before because he was the guy Ryan sent images to if he wanted a second opinion. Dr. Cramer gets a consultant fee, but he doesn't charge a lot, so Ryan can keep the fees down. Hearing some of the billing nightmares some of his clients faced at other clinics made me angry. One woman had been billed over thirty thousand dollars to keep her pug alive for an extra six weeks with painful surgeries to remove tumors and part of a lung, and finally, the poor thing had to be placed on a ventilator, where it spent the last week of its life sedated.

Ryan would have never recommended such an expensive and invasive course of treatment for a terminal creature. He would have strongly recommended comfort measures until it was time to say goodbye, and if she'd insisted on more extreme measures, he would have referred her elsewhere. Some people, whether it was with pets or people, struggled to let go, sometimes to the detriment of the ones they loved. I knew this because Ryan had told me so in confidence.

"Well, hello, Lily," Dr. Cramer said when I got to class. He was robust and physically fit for his age, which I guessed to be early seventies. He had white hair, but it was still thick and healthy, no thinning. "I saw you were on my roster. How's the pup?"

I knew he wasn't talking about Smooshie. Dr.

Cramer was hands-on when it came to reading x-rays, which is why home delivery of the printed images had been required. I'd delivered three of them to him at his home office last week on a beagle who'd been hit by a car. There'd been no doubt his hip had been fractured, but Ryan had been worried about the cervical spine as well, and he wanted a second opinion. There had been a small bone fragment broken loose and the dog had needed surgery. Dr. Cramer had shown me on the images where he'd found it and how he'd recognized the anomaly. If he taught class in the same way, this was going to be a really interesting course.

"Pepper is doing great," I told him. The beagle had made it through with flying colors, and thanks to Dr. Cramer and Ryan, it wouldn't suffer any extra complications from the injury.

His bushy gray brows settled over kind eyes, and his smile was wide, warm, and infectious. "Wonderful."

The class had only six other students. Two young women who looked to be in their teens still. Three young men who weren't much older, and a guy who appeared to be in his thirties. He wore a wedding band. I smiled. I wasn't the only one reinventing myself.

I took a seat in the second row behind the two girls. Two of the younger guys were at the very back of the class. While the third sat in the row up from them. The older man sat three chairs to my right. Dr. Cramer gazed out at us then said, "Everyone in the back, fill in the front two rows."

The young guys didn't groan or complain, but their

protest was definitely in their body language. I worked to hide my smile.

The class, like most first days, lasted only as long as it took Dr. Cramer to run through the code of conduct rules and the course syllabus. He had a strict absentee policy, even more so than the college's when it came to grading. I made a big star on my copy of the syllabus next to the "for every absence after the first one, you will be dropped a letter grade." It seemed harsh, but I guess if a student had gone through all the trouble to get this far into the program, there was a certain level of commitment expected. We would have lectures on Mondays and lab hours on Wednesdays.

"On Wednesdays we'll meet in the science building, room 208. We share it with the radiology students for several disciplines who meet there during the rest of the week, so please be considerate when using, caring for, and cleaning the equipment. Failure to do so can result in a reduction of your grade."

He paused as he gauged our reactions. I glanced at the married guy. He gave me a half-smile and shrugged nervously. I gave him a half-smile and a shrug back.

Dr. Cramer, seemingly satisfied, continued. "We will be meeting twice at a veterinarian clinic for some practical experience in a work setting. You'll be meeting with Dr. Ryan Petry of the Petry Pet Clinic. It would benefit you all to pay careful attention to his work practices, and the practices of those who work for him. Some of you," he nodded to me, and almost all the eyes in the class turned in my direction, "already know Dr. Petry. He's well-respected among his peers. If you want to impress him and me, then don't get in his way when he's working, be professional, know your stuff. The last two things are applicable for my class as well.

"Read chapters one and two in your textbooks. I'll expect you to be able to demonstrate basic safe practices covered in chapter two in the lab on Wednesday, and next Monday, we'll cover the physics of x-rays." He scanned us again. "Any questions?"

One of the young girls, a stout blonde named Bethany, raised her hand.

"Go ahead," Dr. Cramer told her.

"Do we need to buy special clothing for the lab days? Like a lab coat?"

It was a good question.

"No." He looked down at her flip-flops. "But you must wear closed-toe shoes in the lab. Don't want any heavy equipment or chemicals dropped onto your toes. Also, the lab can get cold, so I suggest you all dress appropriately."

I made another note on my syllabus to wear tennis shoes, bring a sweater, and wear long pants.

After he dismissed us, I couldn't stop thinking about the fact that we'd be sharing the lab with radiology students. I stopped by his desk. "Dr. Cramer?"

"Can I help you with something, Lily?"

"Do you know Dale Rogers from the hospital?"

His bushy brows lowered at me. "Do you think all radiologists know each other?"

The way he said it made me laugh. "The fact that you know he's a radiologist tells me it's probably true."

"In a small town like Moonrise, you're not wrong.

Dale and I cross paths here at the college, but rarely anywhere else. Why are you asking about him?" His eyes crinkled for a moment as a pinch of disappointment colored his expression. "You're not involved with him, are you?"

"No," I said quickly. "That's not why I'm asking about him."

"Then why?"

"His ex-wife Abby. She was a friend of mine," I lied. "Recent friend." Less of a lie. "I didn't know her when she was married to Dale. The police think she might have committed suicide, and I can't believe it of the Abby I knew."

"I'm sorry about your friend. I know Dale enough to say hello to him in the hall. I'm afraid I can't help you, Lily, with the answers you're looking for."

I nodded. "I understand." I hadn't expected any real insight from Dr. Cramer. "I hope I didn't make you uncomfortable by asking."

He smiled again. "Of course not." He paused for a moment, much as he had in class when going through the syllabus, then said, "His office is in the science building on the first floor. He's here on Monday mornings, you know, if you just happened to be passing by that way, oh, I don't know, say, to check out where the Wednesday lab is held."

"Thank you, Dr. Cramer."

"See you on Wednesday," he replied on a wink.

THE SCIENCE BUILDING WAS ONE BUILDING OVER. I MADE short work of the walk over, afraid that if I dawdled, I'd miss my chance to check out Dale Rogers. The aroma of chemicals, sour, stringent, and medicinal, wafted in the halls, clinging to the clothes of students exiting labs. There were a lot of rooms on the first floor, and since Dr. Cramer hadn't specified which one was Rogers' office, I took a peek in each one. The first five rooms were class-rooms, but the next two were offices. There were names written on paper and slid into slots near the doors. Lazenby and Donaldson were on one door. The other had Rogers and Daltry written in. This was the place.

I heard talking behind the door, so I paused just outside in the hall and focused my listening.

"I won't talk to you about Abigail," I heard a man say. "Not here. It's not the appropriate time or place."

"Then where would you suggest we talk, Mr. Rogers?" another man asked. I recognized the tonality and authority in the voice. It was acting sheriff Bobby Morris. "We can do this down at the station, if you like? I can arrange that."

"Doctor Rogers," Dale Rogers corrected. After a few seconds of silence, in which I was certain he was being stared down, Rogers said, "Fine. Ask your questions. Anything to get you to go away."

I moved closer to the door, no longer concerned whether someone saw me lurking or not.

"Your wife had an insurance policy."

"My ex-wife," Dale said. "Why does this concern me? We've been divorced for over a year."

"You are named her benefactor, sir," Bobby said. "Don't you think that's strange?"

"Do I think it's strange that my ex," he emphasized ex, "was absent-minded enough to forget to take me off her life insurance policy? No. I don't think it's strange at all. Abby wasn't...reliable."

I kind of agreed with Dale on this one. If Abby had insurance before the divorce, she could have easily forgotten to take his name off as beneficiary. Especially if the payments were automatic. Out of sight, out of mind sort of thing.

"So, you admit you're the one who arranged the life insurance policy."

"She was my wife at the time, so, yes, I admit it. But that has nothing to do with my life now."

Then Bobby Morris dropped the mike. "What about the fact that all the payments have been coming out of your bank account? A five-hundred-thousand-dollar policy is a pretty big motive, don't you think?"

I imagined Dale's face getting red as Bobby slammed him with the facts.

Dale sputtered the next words. "I didn't...I couldn't. I didn't kill Abby. I love her. I wouldn't do that to her." That wasn't a complete lie, but I could feel the edge of untruth in his words. I heard him scoff. "All I can think is that I must have forgotten to take her insurance off automatic payments."

"You loved her enough to leave her with nothing from the divorce settlement. I've seen the court records, Mr. Rogers." Bobby had Rogers on the ropes, and he wasn't about to let up.

"That was an agreement between the two of us," Dale hissed.

"And how did you get her to make this agreement? Did you threaten her?"

"No," he said. "Absolutely not."

For the first time since I'd started eavesdropping, Dale Rogers had told a bald-faced lie. My magical polygraph was pinging off the paper.

"Besides," Dale said, "I wasn't in town two nights ago."

"Where were you?"

I held my breath, waiting for Dale's response.

"Can I help you?" a woman said from behind me. I stumbled back and turned to find myself facing down a very stern-looking black woman. She wore a blue pantsuit, and had her arms crossed over her chest. Her heeled foot tapped against the hall tile as she waited for me to answer.

"Uhm, no, ma'am. I was just looking for my classroom."

"Uh huh." She looked unconvinced. "What class would that be?"

I dropped my backpack down and rummaged through until I found my class roster. "I have Veterinarian Diagnostic Imaging labs on Wednesday. Dr. Cramer doesn't put up with lateness, so I thought I should figure out where the class is so I can find it fast."

Her expression softened, though her eyes still held a hint of suspicion. "You are one floor off," she said. "Room 208 is up those stairs." She pointed to an opening about twenty feet past the offices. "You go up one flight, take a right. Room 208 is the second room on the left."

"Thank you," I said with real relief. I heard the rattle of Rogers' door and inwardly groaned. "I'll head up there now."

She must have seen something in my face, because she said, "Just hold on there a minute."

The door was opening. Crap. Crap. "I really can't. I have another class I have to get to soon."

"What's your name?" She tried to look at my class roster again, but I shoved it in my bag and zipped it up.

"Thanks for all your help." I turned on my heel, trying to walk away before—

"Lily Mason? Is that you?" a man asked.

I turned to face him. Bobby Morris was a tall black man, maybe six feet, four inches in height, with dark skin and warm brown eyes. He wore a brown uniform, crisply pressed. "Oh, hey, Sheriff Morris. What are you doing here?"

The woman who'd caught me listening narrowed her gaze on me. I grimaced.

A man in tan slacks and a blue shirt walked out of the office, red faced and sweating. He appeared to be in his mid-thirties, dark brown hair, glasses, and a thin mustache. He took his glasses off and wiped them with an alcohol wipe, then put them back on before briskly passing us in the hall. He didn't look up or make eye contact with any of us.

Bobby crossed his arms. "Why is it that the only time I see you is when there's a body involved?" he asked.

Now it was the woman's turn to grimace. She gave me a pitiable look then walked away. I guess she figured law enforcement outranked professor.

After she left, I gave him a sly smile. "Just lucky I guess."

"Walk me out," he said.

As we made our way toward the exit, he said in a low voice, "Lord, Lily. Don't tell me you're over here investigating Dale Rogers."

"Okay," I told him. "I am not here investigating Dale Rogers."

"Are you lying?"

"Yes. Well, no. Not really. I'm more interested in what happened to Abby Rogers. So, really, I'm not investigating her ex so much as tracking down leads."

"That's my job, you know." He wasn't angry with me. Bobby and I had worked together before when the previous sheriff had been suspected of corruption. He knew I had value. "What do you think you know?"

"I know that Dale Rogers lied to you about not threatening Abby."

"You were eavesdropping at the door and heard me talking to him."

I nodded, confirming his statement. "I couldn't help it. It's not like you all were being quiet." That was a small lie, but I couldn't explain to him that I had supernatural hearing.

"I should have known you were involved when Nadine asked to revisit the victim's apartment and Reggie called with an inconclusive, possibly suspicious, death report. You three are about as subtle as wrecking balls."

"At least we're not as destructive."

He cocked a brow at me.

"How are the kids?" I asked, changing the subject. Bobby loved talking about his boys.

"Ray made pitcher on his baseball team. Conner just started fourth grade and they are moving him up a reading level."

"What about Billy?" Billy was Bobby's middle child.

Bobby laughed. "Let's just say it's a good thing he's pretty like his mamma."

"Bobby!" Our conversation was easy as we headed out toward the parking lot. My relationship with Sheriff Avery had been contentious and volatile, mostly because Avery had cared more about appearances and being right than he'd cared about the truth. Bobby Morris wasn't like that. He was a good man, and I hoped the town could see that he was the right person for the job when election time rolled around.

"My truck is that way," I said, pointing toward student parking. "Bobby, what is Dale's alibi?" I hadn't heard.

"Now, Lily. You know I can't discuss police business with a civilian."

"Oh, but a civilian can discuss her theories with you?"

He held his hands palms up. "That's the rules. I don't make 'em. I just live by 'em."

I rolled my eyes.

Bobby chuckled. "Stay out of trouble, Lily," he said.

I saluted him with two fingers. "You got it, Sheriff Morris."

The morning had been productive. Dale Rogers had a motive to the tune of five hundred thousand dollars, and money had a way of making people do things they never thought they would. Although, he'd been surprised when Bobby had confronted him about paying for the insurance. But he'd lied about threatening her. Still, did all that make him a murderer? Maybe. There were still other leads to look at, but right now, Dale was at the top of my list.

CHAPTER 11

I had an hour and a half to kill before I had to check in at Petry's Pet Clinic for my afternoon internship. I'd moved my days to Monday and Wednesday afternoons to work best with my class schedule. Ninety minutes wasn't long, but it would be enough time to stop at Reggie's surgical practice and see if she'd gotten any of the blood work back.

It was a clinic day, not a surgery day, so almost every slot in the small parking lot was filled. I picked the first spot available and parked the truck. Nancy, the medical secretary, smiled when she saw me walk in.

I approached the desk.

"Hi, Lily." She looked at her screen for a moment then back to me. "Was Doc expecting you? She has three more consultations before lunch is blocked off for an hour."

"I'm not here for lunch," I said. "I was hoping I could just get a quick word with her between patients."

"I'll have Roberta ask her."

Roberta, an LPN, had just recently replaced Reggie's last nurse who had moved on to a full-time position at the hospital.

I looked around for Margot, the office manager, but she wasn't visible. "Where's Margot today?"

Nancy looked over her shoulder. "She's around here somewhere."

"Can you ask her if she has a minute to talk?" Reggie had said Margot was well-versed in hospital gossip. I really wanted to know who Abby's secret married lover was, because even though he didn't have a name, the guy was at the top of my suspect list along with Dale.

The briefest hint of annoyance flickered in Jan's expression before she nodded, got up from her seat, and walked into the back.

There were five people in the waiting area. One man had a walker, one guy wore a back brace, there was a middle-aged couple watching a talk show on the television in the waiting area, and a younger woman, maybe in her late twenties, early thirties, sat in the corner with her phone on her lap and earbuds in. Since Reggie only had three consults before lunch, some of these folks were here to see one of the other doctor's in her practice.

Nancy came back to the desk. "Margot says you can come on back."

"Thank you, Jan."

She forced a smile. "You're welcome, Lily."

I walked through the clinic door and headed to the end of the first hall. There were two initial rooms, one for vital signs, weight and height, and the next was for lab draw. There was a basket with urine samples and other items that needed to be sent off for analysis. I walked on back to Margot's office. The door was cracked, but I still knocked.

"Come in," she said. Margot was in her fifties, but she looked like she was forty, maybe even younger. She had strawberry-blonde hair that looked very natural, but at her age was probably courtesy of a salon. Even so, she, like Reggie, was always well put together.

"Hi, Margot. I hope you don't mind me dropping in," I said.

"Of course not," she told me. She gestured to a cushioned chair across from her desk. "Have a seat and tell me what I can do for you."

I obliged her. The seat was comfortable. "This is a really great chair," I said.

"I'm glad you like it," Margot said.

I wasn't sure how to bring up Abby's affair, so I started with the obvious. "Terrible, just terrible what happened with Abby Rogers. She was a good nurse."

Margot's expression turned sympathetic. "She was capable." The way Margot said the word made it sound like high praise.

"Yes," I agreed solemnly. "I just recently met her, but she seemed like she knew what she was doing."

"When it came to medicine, she absolutely did. Abby had been at the top of her class."

"And outside of medicine?"

Margot stared at me for a minute. "What did you want to see me about again?"

I heard a snort from the doorway as Reggie joined us. "She wants to know what you can tell her about Abby Rogers' personal life because she doesn't think the girl killed herself."

"Oh," Margot said. Her forehead wrinkled when she frowned, adding age to her face. "And what do you think, Dr. Crawford?"

"I don't," she said. "I let the medical findings speak for me."

Margot shook her head. "I hate to speak ill of the dead."

Didn't everyone? It's amazing how wonderful some jerks became in the eyes of the living once they perished from this existence.

"I'm not trying to judge Abby. Whatever you tell me won't stop me from trying to find the truth about what happened to her. And while it can't bring her any peace, not anymore, it might offer some to her family and friends."

"What about you, Dr. Crawford? Are you okay with this?"

Reggie nodded. "I investigate my way. Lily investigates hers. Whatever you tell her won't change the evidence, but it might give us other places to look."

"All right, then," Margot said. "Abby was having an affair with a married doctor."

I scooted forward in my seat. I was finally going to hear a name. "Which one?"

"Oh." Margot blinked. "I don't know. They were

very good at hiding the affair."

It seemed like everyone knew about the affair, but no one knew who the mysterious married doctor was. "Well, shoot. How did you find out about the affair, if you don't mind me asking?"

"I overheard Dr. Rogers talking about his divorce to one of the other doctors at the hospital." Apparently, I wasn't the only one in the room who liked to eavesdrop.

"Do you think he knows who Abby was seeing?"

"Absolutely," Margot said. "The other doctor asked him who it was, and Dr. Rogers said he'd signed some agreement, so he couldn't say, or he would forfeit everything he got in the divorce settlement."

Interesting.

"What a piece of trash," Reggie said. "He black-mailed that poor girl into signing over half of everything she was due."

Margot nodded. "That's what I gathered from the conversation. The settlement was contingent on him keeping his trap shut.

"It didn't stop him from trying to ruin her reputation, though, did it?" Anger for Abby settled in me. She might have been having an affair, and maybe Dale did or didn't deserve her disloyalty, but he'd gotten what he wanted. A divorce that he didn't have to pay for. So why take that one step extra to hurt her even more? "What doctor was he talking to?" Maybe Rogers had told him more out of Margot's earshot.

"Smith," she said. "Dr. Stewart Smith."

AFTER I LEFT REGGIE'S, I STILL HAD OVER FORTY MINUTES before I had to be at Petry's Pet Clinic, so I decided to stop by Moonrise Manor and check on Opal.

The parking lot, much like the surgical services' parking lot, was packed. I expected it to be busier on a weekday than a weekend, but I'd been here on Friday as well, and there were less than half the vehicles that were here now. Maybe Monday was a big family visitor day, or maybe I'd picked a time when an event was taking place. Either way, I once again took the first spot available and made the long walk to the front entrance.

In the hall across from the main office, Annie Blankenship was sitting in front of a stack of folders, her face pinched and red with stress, sweat beading on her upper lip, as she read through the one she had opened. Inside the office, the director of nursing and the administrator huddled with the social worker and a few other people I didn't recognize. The halls were buzzing with activity, residents were up and outside their rooms, most of them looking confused as to why.

I kept my head down until I got to Opal's room. She was swatting Mariah, the aide, away from her. "I can get myself dressed," Opal said. "Stop fussing with me." She held up the pants. They were pale-blue, thick polyester. "These aren't even my clothes? Where are my pants?"

"I'm sorry, Ms. Dixon. These didn't have a name in them, so we thought they might be your size."

"Do they look like something I'd wear? I'm seventy-six, not a hundred and seventy-six."

"I couldn't find anything else clean."

"I'm not wearing some other lady's pants. I'll go naked first," Opal said.

Mariah looked back and saw me standing in the door. She looked almost as stressed as the woman with the files.

"Get in here," Opal said to me. "And get this girl to leave me alone."

"What's happening?" I asked Mariah. "Aside from the clothing debacle. Things are nuts out in the hall."

"The state has come down to inspect the nursing home," she said. Her eyes bugged. "I shouldn't have said that."

"It's okay. Do you know why?"

Mariah shook her head. "They can pop in randomly for a spot inspection. Sometimes it's because a complaint has been called in."

"Do you think this is random or was there a complaint?"

"Honestly, I don't know." She took a few steps back from Opal. "I have to get to the next room. Can you please talk her into getting dressed and going down for lunch?"

"I'll try." I looked at Opal. I had a feeling she was going to go down for lunch or not as she felt like it. I noticed Jane's bed was empty and neatly made. "Where's Mrs. Davidson?"

"She's in the hospital for a few days. They're trying

to figure out why her diabetes is acting so weird," Opal said. She glared at Mariah. "You can go."

Mariah sighed, not nearly as relaxed as she'd been about Opal's cantankerous ways on Friday, then walked right out without looking back.

"What in the world is going on?" I asked Opal. "It's a madhouse out there."

"I'm pretty sure this has something to do with Abby. I overheard one of the other nurses say that Abby might have put in a call to state last week."

"About what? Do you know?"

Opal shook her head. "I think it has something to do with Jane Davidson, though."

"What gives you that idea?"

"Because a woman came in with a big ol' clipboard and asked me a half dozen questions about the care I was receiving, and then turned around and asked me a hundred questions about Jane."

"Wow." I mulled it over for a moment. "Do you think Abby reported something about Mrs. Davidson then? Something about her care?" What was it she'd been trying to get done on Friday? I snapped my fingers. "She had asked Dr. Smith about getting some tests run on Mrs. Davidson, and he had been snappish, but finally agreed."

"Female Dr. Smith or male Dr. Smith?"

"Male," I replied.

"He's a jackass," Opal said. "His wife, though, she's a saint. Have to be to put up with that fool." She patted her hip. "The woman fixed me right up."

Right. Reggie had told me the female Dr. Smith was an orthopedic surgeon. But…

"How do you know the male Dr. Smith? Is he your doctor here?"

"Not hardly," Opal said. Her mouth thinned as she met my gaze. "I'm pretty sure he's the one Abby had the affair with."

CHAPTER 12

The afternoon at the clinic moved at a snail's pace. Not that it wasn't busy. Monday was the day all the worried pet parents who hadn't wanted to face an "emergency visit" fee over the weekend showed up bright and early as drop-ins.

Ryan made a practice of allowing walk-ins on the understanding that true emergencies and booked appointments took priority. The rest might have to wait a while to get worked in. A grumpy-looking, bald-headed man wearing coveralls sat with a large St. Bernard. Kelly, the VAT, told me the dog had eaten a roll of toilet paper Friday night and had stopped eating yesterday, and he hadn't had a bowel movement to pass the paper yet.

"Toilet paper," she said, taking her ginger hair out of its ponytail, combing it back with her fingers, and reapplying the hair tie with practiced quickness, "will stop up more than a toilet. In bulk, it can swell when it starts to absorb the water from the stomach and intestines."

"What can be done for him?"

"We've done an ultrasound to determine the blockage exists. Unfortunately, surgical intervention at this point is necessary," she said. "We've cancelled a few routine appointments this afternoon, so it can be performed right away."

No wonder the bald man looked grumpy. He was probably worried, too. I know I would be. It was just sheer luck that Smooshie hadn't ended up with the same problem when she ate one of my sanitary pads. Well, a part of one. And no, it wasn't used. Ugh. I'd talked to Ryan, and he'd said as long as she was eating, staying hydrated, and having regular bowel movements, that she would be fine. Well, Smooshie had pooped confetti for a few days, but other than that, she'd suffered no ill effects. Like I said, luck.

"Mr. Donovan, I can take Bernie back now," Kelly said to the man. She walked over and took the big dog's leash. She gave Bernie's dad a sympathetic look. "Dogs eat stuff they shouldn't. It's not your fault."

"I should have brought him in sooner," Mr. Donovan said.

Kelly shook her head. "It would have been the same result." She gave Bernie a neck scratch. "Don't you worry. Dr. Ryan will take good care of him, okay?"

"You'll call me as soon as the surgery is over?"

"I will," Kelly said. "I will call you immediately."

Kelly had a way with people that helped set them at ease, including this lowly intern. When we escorted Bernie to the back, I told her so. "You're really good at making people feel better."

"Why, thanks, Lily. That's sweet of you to say."

"It's just the truth."

She smiled and shook her head. "I just imagine that everyone who walks through the door is me with my Diva. She's my labradoodle. I think about how I would feel if she were sick, and how I would want to be treated and talked to. They're scared. I'd be scared, too, and I work here. If you approach everyone from that perspective, then you find yourself saying things that would make you feel better if you were in that situation."

"You're right. Every time Smooshie drinks too fast and chokes on water, I worry she's going to aspirate into her lungs and get pneumonia." I spent so much time at the rescue where the pet owners were the bad guys, that sometimes it was hard to switch off that feeling.

My phone, in the front pocket of my lab coat, rang. I gave Kelly an apologetic smile before taking it out. It was a local number, but one I didn't recognize. I declined the call, forcing it to go to voice mail. If it was one of the gazillion spam calls that I received every week, they wouldn't leave a message.

The phone rang out with three successive beeps, alerting me that a message had indeed been left. I opened my voice mail and was surprised by the caller.

Hi, Lily. This is Lacy. Lacy Evans, Freda's daughter. The explanation was longer than it needed to be. She went on. *Opal Dixon is leaving Moonrise Manor against medical advice. We can't stop her, because she's here voluntarily. She asked me to call you. She says you can either come and get her, or she's going to start walking.*

I wondered how far Opal could get with a broken leg and a walker. Probably not a good idea to find out.

Ryan walked out of one of the exam rooms. He gave me a strange look. "Are you okay?"

I shook my head and replayed him the message. He was actually grinning at the end.

"That Opal is a pistol," he said.

"Opal owns a pistol, and she's about to shoot her own foot off."

"Nah," Ryan said. "She'd probably do fine at her place with some home health care. A nurse can come out once or twice a week to check on the surgical wound, and physical therapy will come out two or three days a week to work at getting her stronger." He shrugged. "A lift on the toilet, a shower chair. She wouldn't need much."

"They already have a shower chair," I said, flashing back to Pearl straddling Bob. I shook my head. "Do you mind if I cut my hours short today?"

"Nope," he said. "Go help Opal stage her prison break."

BY THE TIME I'D PULLED UP TO MOONRISE, THE PARKING lot was less packed. Opal sat on a bench just outside the entrance with a white trash bag full of what I could only imagine were her personal effects. I swung the truck into the drive-thru in front of the main entrance.

An area reserved for convenient drop-offs and pick-ups.

She stared at me then pushed up on her good leg and brought herself to a stand. There was no curb to navigate, so she easily used her walker to make her way to the passenger door then shouted at the window. "It's about time you showed up," she groused. "Now, get me out of here."

I got out and walked around to her side. She was already folding the walker. Before I could take it from her, she flung it into the back of the truck.

My eyes widened.

"My leg is broke, not my arms." She flexed a small muscle. "Besides, it's aluminum, so it weighs all of five pounds."

I laughed. "Okay, then. Tell me how to get you into the seat. I mean, if it was your left leg it would be easier, I think. I don't know. I don't have much experience with this kind of thing."

"Don't be useless, Lily." She put her hand on my shoulder. "Just lift me in."

I was definitely strong enough to carry Opal. She wasn't much taller than me, and we probably weighed about the same. My shifter strength, which was only slightly more than that of a strong human male, would make it easy. But could I do it without doing any damage to her injured leg?

Lacy came outside before I could try. "Want some help?"

"Yes," I said eagerly. "Definitely."

Opal shook her head. "Wimp."

"Damn straight," I told her. "Pearl will whoop my butt if I break you. You know, more than you're already broken."

"I don't want to get in trouble here, so why don't we move this along," Lacy said. She opened the door. "Opal, you need to grab the chicken handle." She pointed to the strap attached to the ceiling.

"Chicken handle?" I asked.

Lacy smiled. "That's what my mom always called it when she was teaching me to drive."

I got it. It was the handle you grabbed when the driver scared the pee out of you.

"What next?" Opal asked after she laced her fingers into the handle.

"Luckily, Lily's truck is small, but the seat is still higher than your rear end, so I want you to hold and pull the chicken handle with your left hand. Next, you'll push down on the top of the window ledge with your right to support your bad leg while you step up into the truck with your good leg to get in. I'll stand behind you, stabilize the door and guide you in. You only have to get a hip on the seat then scoot in. Sounds easy enough, right?"

"That sounds super easy," she said with a lot of sarcasm.

It only took one try, with an extra assist from Lacy, and Opal was safely seated in my truck and putting her seat belt on.

"Thanks, Lacy," I said. "I appreciate you calling and the extra help."

"Opal and Pearl helped my mom and me when I was pregnant."

Opal stared straight ahead as if she hadn't heard Lacy.

I focused back on the young mom.

She said, "They gave her extra-large tips, sometimes more than double what they'd paid for lunch when money was at its tightest. Mom knew what they were doing, and she appreciated that they'd never made her feel like a charity case. Now that I'm a little older, I can appreciate it as well."

Opal grunted. That was all the reply Lacy was going to get.

"I better get back inside. I have a med pass before my shift ends."

I nodded, then asked, "Did they ever figure out how Mrs. Davidson's blood sugar dropped so low?"

"The doctors have no idea. She's been a type one diabetic since she was seventeen years old. It's not as if her pancreas can suddenly start producing its own insulin."

"Could it have been a medication error?" I asked.

"The nurses are the ones who give the injections. That would have been Rick."

"You gave her the glucagon shot," I said.

"I can administer live-saving injections, like epinephrine for acute allergic reactions that involve the airway and the glucagon for severe hypoglycemia. But if she'd been conscious or her blood sugar had been over forty, I would have gotten Rick to assess and evaluate. I can't see him making a mistake with her insulin, but I'll look into it." She glanced over her shoulder at the door. "I really need to get back inside. I need this job to pay for school."

"Can we talk tonight?" I asked. "About Abby, I mean. I know you live in her apartment building."

Lacy hesitated, then nodded. "Stop by around eight-thirty. I'll have put Paulie to bed by then. I'll tell you what I know."

When I got into the truck, I grabbed my phone.

"Now is not the time to be making phone calls," Opal said.

"I'm just going to call Pearl and give her a heads up that we're coming." The shower scene the last time I showed up at the Dixon residence played in my head. "It's the polite thing to do."

CHAPTER 13

Pearl Dixon was in her yard raking when I dropped off Opal. Audrey the cat was perched in the window watching us. Pearl had been home alone when I'd called, and, though she'd acted irritated, I could tell she was relieved to have Opal home. I'd already told Opal about the home health options Ryan had mentioned, but I repeated it to Pearl so she'd make sure that Opal called her doctor tomorrow to get help arranged.

After I'd made sure they were settled, I headed out to the rescue. For some reason, I really needed to hug my dog. I wanted to hug Parker as well, but Smooshie first. On the way, I called Nadine. "Hey, girl," I said when she answered. "Just wanted to let you know I ran into Bobby at the college today. He was interviewing Dale Rogers."

"I heard," Nadine said, sounding amused. "I don't think Bobby knows what to make of you most of the time, but at least he's not a jerk about it like Avery."

"So, are you going to tell me if you found anything at Abby's apartment? I know you got to search it again."

"You were there. I found the same things you found. Except for the cat, of course. I can't believe Larry didn't notice that there might be a cat in the apartment. What a bonehead."

"How'd he take being usurped on the case?"

"He couldn't care less. He's convinced it's a suicide, and that we're all spinning our wheels. I hope he's not right."

"He's wrong," I told her. "Also, I found out who Abby was having the affair with."

"Tell me already."

"It was Smith."

"The orthopedic doctor? She set my arm for me a few years ago. I wouldn't have guessed she swung both ways."

"Not her," I said. "Him."

"I figured," Nadine said. "I was just trying to spice it up a little. Did you get this from Reggie?"

"Nope. Margot was clueless. I'm beginning to suspect she might even be the source of the gossip about the affair, and the reason no one really knew anything is because *she* didn't. She'd heard just enough to be dangerous, but not enough to be helpful. Opal told me."

"Why, that stinker," Nadine huffed. "I can't believe she knew and didn't tell us sooner."

"She was trying to protect Abby from gossip, and

she didn't think the old affair had anything to do with her death."

Nadine gave me a look and said, "Uh huh, sure."

"You, know, I'd do it for you if anything ever happened."

"Damn right," Nadine said. "Wipe the computer history and burn the porn stash."

I choked out a laugh. "You don't really have a porn stash, do you?" I asked with real interest.

"Nope," she answered. I could hear the wink in her voice. "Again, just trying to keep it spicy."

"Lacy told me I could stop by her place tonight around eight-thirty. Maybe we should grab Reggie and a bottle of wine and make it a girls' night."

Nadine laughed this time. "You hate wine."

"I don't hate it. I would call it more of a strong dislike." I much preferred beer. "We can grab a six pack as well."

"I'll call Reggie," she said. "I'll swing by and pick you up around eight. Get a babysitter."

"Smooshie will be so disappointed, Auntie Nadine."

Nadine chuckled. "She'll get over it."

I hung up with my friend about the same time I arrived at the shelter. We had a great big parking lot now, so I pulled in next to Parker's big black dually pickup. The extended bed stuck out a good five feet past my bumper. I wasn't sure anyone needed a truck that size, but he really loved his vehicle, so who was I to judge.

When I got out, I was surprised to see Michael

Lowell, who I recognized from his friend page picture, walking out of the front office.

"You're Lily, right?" he asked as I approached his location on the sidewalk.

"I am," I said. "Can I help you?"

"My name is Michael Lowell," he said.

The cougar in me couldn't help but size him up to evaluate his threat level. The guy was thin with short blond hair, and he was of average height, at about five feet, ten inches. He had a lean body that looked built for things like walking and yoga, not fighting.

"Hello, Michael Lowell." I had wanted to talk to Michael about his involvement with Abby, but him showing up at my work gave me a creeping vibe. Maybe his appearance had nothing to do with me or Abby. Maybe he was looking to add a new family member to his household. "Are you looking to adopt a dog?"

"I wasn't," he admitted. "But Parker Knowles has a way of changing your mind. I've always loved animals, but I'm not sure about the responsibility." He glanced back at the office door. "I signed up to volunteer."

"That's great. It's a good way to get your feet wet, especially for animal lovers who have never kept pets."

He nodded. "I actually came out here to see *you*."

"Why ever for?" I hoped it had nothing to do with Nadine sending him a friend request on my behalf. As far as I knew, it wasn't a dating app.

"You saved my mimi," he said. "I just wanted to thank you personally."

"Your mimi?"

"I'm ridiculous," he said. "My grandma. Mimi is what I call my grandma. Jane Davidson," he added.

"Oh, right. Mrs. Davidson." I nodded. "How is she doing? I asked today at the home, and they said she's still in the hospital."

"Her blood sugar has been holding steady since the incident. They are still waiting to see if she might have any neurological deficits. But she seems to be coming around. A blood sugar that low can cause some brain damage. I'm praying she'll be okay. The doctors are baffled. Frankly," he said, "so am I. Mimi has always been good about regulating her blood sugar. She's had to deal with it her entire life."

I remembered he'd made her candy. "What's in the caramels that you make her?" I asked.

He gawked at me. "Nothing that would cause her blood sugar to drop," he said. "And nothing to shoot it up too high. The recipe is from a diabetes cookbook. Mimi used to make them for herself until she ended up in that place." He fairly spat out the last word.

"How long has she been there?"

"A year and one month," he said. "She had been living with my parents, but she stopped being able to do a lot of stuff for herself."

"That's a hard decision to make."

"I don't blame my folks," he said swiftly. "It's just been hard on Mimi. On everyone."

"I'm sure." I tried to employ Kelly's technique of imagining if it were me. If my grandparent or parent had gotten to an age where it was impossible to keep him or her home, and I had to place them in nursing care. How would I feel? Helpless? Angry? Guilty? All of the above, probably. "She seems to like it there okay."

"Mimi puts on a brave face." He frowned. "Or at least I thought so." He rubbed his arms as if suddenly chilled. "Anyway, I saw on your profile that you worked here at the pit bull rescue. I looked the place up on the internet and brought some supplies that were on the wish list as a way to say thank you for your intervention on Mimi's behalf. As low as her blood sugar got, I'm praying she doesn't have brain damage."

"Bringing supplies was really nice of you." Pearl had said nice was the kiss of death for Abby. "I was sure sorry to hear about Abby Rogers," I said. "Your grandma told me you all were dating."

"Abby was a sweet girl, but we only went out twice. Mimi really liked her, so she hoped it would be more. I think Abby was still in love with her ex."

"Dale Rogers?"

Michael shrugged. "She was single but not available. You know what I mean."

I did. During the four months I'd waited for Parker to decide if he could handle my less-than-human status, I'd been "single but not available." That's the way it was when you loved someone, but you couldn't be with them. "Did she have anyone she was afraid of? Anything that might have given you the idea that she might be in danger?"

He shook his head. "Honestly, I only knew her as well as someone can know a person after a couple of encounters." He smiled. "I better get going. I promised Mimi I'd come see her tonight."

"Do you know if Abby thought anything wrong was going on at the manor? Any resident neglect?"

He looked off into the distance for a moment as he sorted through his memories. "I'm not sure." Then he held up a finger. "Our second date, she did ask me something strange."

"What's that?"

"She wanted to know if I ever felt like Mimi's medical needs were not being met."

"Did she mention anything specific?"

Michael shook his head. "No. I got the idea she had something particular in mind, but when I pressed her to explain, she said she'd just been curious. Mimi had developed sores on her toes, but other than that, it seems like they do a good job at taking care of her." He shook his head. "I don't know. It just struck me as a strange question to ask."

I nodded. "Well, I won't keep you, Michael. Thank you for the supplies and tell your grandma that I'm glad she's recovering."

He nodded. I heard a beep at his waist. He lifted his shirt and tapped a button on the side of a small device about the size of my phone.

"What's that?" I said.

"My insulin pump. It monitors my blood glucose levels and gives me insulin as I need it."

"You're diabetic?"

He nodded. "It runs in the family."

"Wow. You have to wear that all the time?"

"Since I was a teenager. Though, the insulin pumps

have gotten better over time. It used to really bother me, but I'm used to it now."

"That's why you make diabetic candy."

He grinned. "Mimi's not the only one with a sweet tooth."

I decided I liked Michael Lowell. He loved his grandma and he'd been honest during our conversation. "It's nice to meet you, Michael. Please give your mimi my best regards."

"I'll do just that," he said.

Robyn Patterson walked out an enclosed access door with Jolly, a tan mastiff-pit bull mix, into a fenced-in area in front of the rescue. Michael smiled at her. Robyn waved before starting a game of fetch with Jolly. Michael laughed as Jolly launched himself in the air.

"Do you want to come and play with us?" Robyn said, her voice a little flirty.

Michael glanced at me, and I gave him an *it's up to you* shrug.

"Mimi won't mind waiting a little bit." He was transfixed, and I wasn't sure if it was because of Jolly or Robyn or both. Either way, I think Michael was well on his way to becoming a pit bull lover like the rest of us.

Since there was no access through the gate from outside, I tapped his arm to get his attention. "Come on," I told him. "I'll take you through to play area one."

CHAPTER 14

Nadine called me when she and Reggie were on their way. I'd showered and changed at Parker's. He and his dad were going to have dinner together at the house. I hoped that meant Greer was finally going to tell Parker about the engagement. It had been hard not to spill the beans about the news last night while we were all together. Unfortunately, it wasn't my business to tell, so I kept my mouth shut.

Still, it had been harder than I'd thought, knowing something I couldn't tell Parker. I didn't want to keep any secrets from him ever again. Which is why I'd told him about Stewart Smith and Abby, and Bobby's questioning of Dale, and Abby's mom saying she had a persistent new boyfriend, even though I didn't think it was Michael Lowell; he hadn't given me a stalker vibe. And I didn't leave out the fact that a state inspection team had been scouring the nursing home, and that Abby had potentially made the call that got them there.

All in all, it was a lot of noise but not a lot of sense. It was like someone emptied several puzzles onto the floor then mixed them all up, grabbed several handfuls, put them back in the box, and said, "Solve this." It seemed and felt impossible, and I couldn't help but feel like I was missing something in all these mismatched fragments.

I hoped our conversation with Lacy would prove to be the catalyst that brought all the pieces together.

When the girls arrived, I climbed into the back of Nadine's car. It was a two-door sports coupe, and climbing in and out of the backseat seemed more of a me thing than a Reggie thing. Besides, I didn't mind. I used my phone as a flashlight while I sorted through some photos of Abby's apartment that Nadine had brought along for show and tell.

"The IT lady went through Abby's laptop. It wasn't hard to crack the password."

"Let me guess. Audrey?"

"Close," Nadine said. "It was the capital letter I, less-than symbol, the number three, and then Audrey with a capital A. You know, like I heart Audrey."

"I get it." Although I would never have guessed. My password was my brother's birthday and his initials. I didn't tend to vary it up too much unless the website I was logging into made me. Thankfully, my subscriptions were limited to less than a handful. "Did they find anything interesting?"

"We're not sure, yet. There wasn't a suicide note, much to Larry's disappointment. She had been looking up lab results though, blood work and such that would indicate cancer and diseases."

"Did Abby have cancer?" I asked.

"Not that I could find," Reggie said. She was a healthy thirty-year-old."

"Except for the being dead part," Nadine added.

"Yes, except for that."

As I scanned the pictures, I couldn't help but feel like the photos were wrong somehow, but I couldn't quite put my finger on it. "You took these today, right?"

"Yes," Nadine said. "Got there around nine this morning and we searched until just before noon. I wish I could say we saw more, but if your eyes and nose couldn't pick up any clues, I don't know what hope we mere mortals had." There was a dramatic pause before she amended, "You know, because you just seem to have a sixth-sense for these things." She glanced sideways at Reggie, who had barely taken notice of her statement, then in the rearview mirror at me.

Smooth, I thought. A couple weeks in a place full of therianthropic shifters had probably made her less guarded about her knowledge. She'd have to readjust her thinking if she was going to keep our secret. Though I supposed it was now her and Parker's secret, as well. They had a lot to lose if the wrong people found out, just like me and my uncle.

"Did you guys move anything around in the rooms before you took these pictures?" I asked. There were numbers next to all the items in the apartment, maybe that's what made them feel off to me, but I didn't think that was it. Something was missing. Something that Pearl and I hadn't taken. Which meant it was removed between Saturday night and this morning.

"No. We didn't start our deep search until everything had been catalogued and photographed. Why?"

"I'm not sure, yet." A lot had happened in the past couple of days, so it was going to have to compare them against the pictures I took to know for sure.

Before I could grab my town, Reggie said, "I got the tox reports back this evening."

"Way to bury the lead!" Nadine said. "How come you didn't tell me when you picked me up?"

"I wanted to wait until after we picked up Lily. That way I wouldn't have to tell it twice."

Nadine stuck her tongue out.

Reggie laughed and gave her a chuck under the chin, and Nadine retracted the appendage.

"Good way to lose a body part," Reggie said. "I used to do that to CeCe when she was little." She sighed wistfully.

"And we want to hear all about how cute your baby was, and all the joys that came with being her mother, but first, lab results," Nadine said.

Every word of the statement had been honest. Nadine wanted to talk about kids with Reggie.

This week's puzzle just added a layer.

"She tested positive for fentanyl," Reggie said.

"Isn't that the opioid that's killing everyone?" Nadine asked.

"It's been responsible for a lot of deaths, but usually because it's mixed with other drugs or illegal substances. Like fentanyl-laced heroin. That's become more popular. I had a colleague at the seminar tell me about two deaths in the past month in Jefferson City related to the lethal mix."

"Did she test positive for heroin?" I asked. "And what about the oxycodone they'd found on her nightstand?"

"No to the heroin or to oxy," Reggie said. "And really, the level of fentanyl in her system wasn't enough to do more than get her a high." She twisted in her seat to look back at me. "I sent off a hair sample for further examination."

"Why?"

"Because I don't believe Abby was a chronic drug user. And if her hair sample doesn't show any drugs in the screen, it will mean the fentanyl was a new thing for her. There's no way, as a nurse, she'd choose fentanyl as her introduction to hard drugs. I just can't see it. Besides, there were none of the telltale signs of drug use. Except for some benign cysts on her ovaries, she was just too healthy. Liver, heart, pancreas, kidney. Heck, even her gallbladder was pristine. Her stomach lining was thick and pink, her intestines had no ulcerations, nothing abnormal, and her brain showed no trauma, tumors, or bleeding."

"Then what caused her death?"

"I wish I knew." Reggie slumped in the seat. "It's confounding. Like getting to the end of a mystery and the last few pages with the reveal are written in a foreign language."

"I know the feeling." Something Reggie said triggered my memory. I flipped through Nadine's photos once more, stopping on one that was of the reading nook in her bedroom. "Speaking of books," I said. "I know what's wrong with this picture."

There had been a book on the stand next to the chair about historical murders, and now it was gone. "Have either of you heard of Kenneth..." What had that last name been again? "Burrough, or something like that?"

"Does he live in Moonrise?" Nadine asked.

"No. Abby had a book about murder bookmarked on her table in her bedroom. It's not in any of these pictures. The chapter she was reading was on a guy named Kenneth Burrough, although the last name isn't quite right."

"What did this Kenneth guy do to get a whole chapter?" Reggie asked.

"I wish I knew. I didn't think it was important. Heck, it still might not be, but I didn't take it, and you said you all didn't move anything before the pictures, so..."

"So, it could be a clue," Nadine agreed. She turned into the Sunset Apartment Complex. "Let's put a pin in it for a second. I'm sure it will come to me as soon as I stop trying to think of the name. Let's go see a girl about some gossip."

"I've got the wine chiller," Reggie said. "A merlot guaranteed to loosen the lips." She patted a thermal-insulated bag that was shaped like a bottle of wine.

"Cute," I said. "Where's the beer?" My lips were as loose as I wanted them.

"In the trunk," Nadine said. "I'll grab it out of the cooler."

While Reggie and I waited for Nadine to get the

beer, I had the strangest sensation of being watched. I scanned the parking area lit up by streetlamps for any lurkers. I didn't see anyone. I kept my back to Reggie and allowed some of my cougar to slip into my eyes, giving my night vision a boost as I studied the area again.

Then I saw it. There was a dark-blue four-door sedan parked across the street from the complex—and in the driver's seat, Opal Dixon was watching us with a pair of binoculars.

She must have lit on my eyes, because she dropped the binoculars, her expression one of surprise. I put away my second nature so when she finally dug them back out of her lap and looked my way again, instead of green, glowing eyes, she'd just see me. If she asked, I'd tell her it was a trick of the light.

I waved at her, and she knew she'd been caught. "Opal is here," I announced.

"Where?" Nadine turned in a circle.

"Just across the street." I pointed at her car.

"Why is she sitting in her car?" Reggie asked.

"I'd imagine because she has a broken leg."

"Smart alec," Nadine said. "I mean, why is she here."

"If I had to hazard a guess, I'd say that Pearl is back in Abby's apartment. She does have a key."

"Cripes." Nadine jogged to the door. "It might not have been a crime scene two days ago, but it is now."

Reggie and I entered the building and looked down the hall. Sure enough, there was crime scene tape on the floor in front of Abby's apartment.

"I'm going to arrest her," Nadine said.

"With a six pack of beer in your hands?" I shook my head. "Let's find out what they're doing here first." Opal and Pearl knew Abby better than most. "Maybe they've thought of something that might help us."

"Or they're burning the porn stash," Nadine said metaphorically.

"And wiping the hard drive," I added.

Reggie frowned. "I'm going to punch you both if you don't start including me in your conversations."

Yikes. Had we been doing that? It was easier to talk to Nadine since she knew the truth, but I never meant for Reggie to feel left out. I draped my arm across her shoulder. "If you die, we promise to destroy any material that might make you look less than the awesomesauce you are." I crossed my heart. Nadine did the same and added some scout salute.

"It's a best friends pact," she said.

Reggie smiled. "Okay, I get it. Porn stash, search history." In a quieter voice, she said, "I have a locked box under my bed. Don't open it. Just get rid of it so that CeCe never has to see."

Nadine rubbed her hands together. "Oooo. Reggie has sex toys. Now I know why Greer popped the question. You're a wild one."

Reggie laughed hard.

"Stop," I told them both. Reggie might be one of my best friends, but Greer was like a second father to me, and no one wanted to think about a parent in compromising positions. "I don't need that image in my head."

The door opposite Abby's opened, and a large

woman with gray hair and wearing a panda-bear-laden robe stepped out into the hall. "You're not the cops," she said with disappointment.

Before she could duck back in, Nadine handed me the beer and said, "I'm Deputy Booth of the Moonrise Sheriff's Department, ma'am. Did you need help?"

Since Nadine was wearing tight blue jeans, cowgirl boots, and a lavender T-shirt, the woman gave her a skeptical scowl. "I'll wait for the real cops, sweetie."

Nadine pulled her wallet out of her purse and flashed her badge. "I *am* a real cop, sweetie," she replied.

"Fine," the woman huffed. "I reported a break-in at my neighbor's. People going in and out at all hours." She pushed her glasses up her nose and took a closer look at Nadine. "Yes. You were here today with those other police. I recognize you now." She peered at me. "And you were here the other night with the old bitty who broke in tonight."

"She has a key," Reggie and I said at the same time. We exchanged sly smiles.

"She tore down that tape the cops had put up there today, so as far as I'm concerned it means you can't go in there." She glowered at Nadine. "Or am I wrong?"

Nadine said, "You're not wrong."

"How do you know when someone is coming and going over there?" I asked.

The woman pointed to her doorbell; the fancy one I'd noticed Saturday night. "It has a motion detector and a camera. When someone walks in front of it, it makes sounds in my house and I can look at the monitor in my living room to see who it is."

I think Nadine's mouth hung as wide as my own. "Ma'am, this information would have been pertinent to our police investigation. Why didn't you come forward before now?"

"Because it was a suicide three days ago. At least that's what that one young deputy told me."

"Shobe," I said.

"That's his name," the lady said. "Didn't seem like what I had to say was of any interest for him."

"What's your name?" Nadine asked.

"Belinda Mitchell," she said.

"Ms. Mitchell, do you happen to save the video you record from your doorbell?"

"Why, yes, Deputy Booth, I do. Or at least the machine does. For two weeks."

The front entrance opened, and Deputy Larry Shobe, in full uniform, walked in. The look on Nadine's face when she saw him made me glad I wasn't him.

"Deputy Booth," he said, his expression confused. "What are you doing here?"

"I'm doing your damn job, Shobe. That's what I'm doing here."

His Adam's apple bobbed as he gulped down hard. "I don't understand."

Nadine nodded. "That's becoming clearer every day." She walked over to Abby's door and pounded on it. "Pearl, get your blue-headed self out here now."

A few seconds passed, then the door opened, and Pearl stepped out, a sheepish look on her face. "Well, hey, girls," she said genially. "I just came by to pick up more cat food for Audrey. She held up a small can of Salmon Supper for cats.

"Go home, Pearl. Now." Nadine pointed to the doors, obviously not buying it. "I'll be by tomorrow for a chat with you and your sister, and you will both tell me everything you know about Abigail Rogers."

To Larry Shobe, she said, "Follow Ms. Mitchell into her house. Take a complete statement, then bag the memory card in her monitor as evidence. And I swear if you so much as do any damage to it, the only cases you will touch from now on will involve illegally parked vehicles, do you get me?"

"Yes, Deputy Booth," he said. He hurriedly followed Belinda Mitchell into her apartment.

"Dang, girl. That was totally boss," Reggie said. "I almost peed my pants."

"Me too," I giggled.

Nadine shook her head. She smiled, but the frown lines were still deep between her eyes. "This case has been mishandled since the beginning. I'm kicking myself for not knocking on every neighbor's door today. You two go on up to Lacy's while I take care of this. We'll put our heads together tomorrow."

I nodded. "It's a plan."

Reggie and I were headed to the stairs when Pearl came jogging through the front doors, her face red and beaded with sweat, and her whole body shaking.

"Opal!" she cried out. "Someone took my sister."

CHAPTER 15

"Are you certain she didn't just drive off?" Nadine asked Pearl for the dozenth time. The hallway had filled up with residents who had heard the commotion in the hall and now wanted a front-row seat to a kidnapping event.

"I'm positive," Pearl said. "I may be old, but I'm not blind. I saw someone get in the passenger side. Opal looked at me before she drove off. She was scared." Pearl wrung her hands until they were cherry red. "The person was in the shadows though, so I can't tell you what they looked like. Why aren't you out there looking for her?"

"We've got every available officer patrolling the streets, and we have an APB out on her car. I promise you, Pearl, we are doing everything we can to bring Opal back to you."

"Deputy Booth," Shobe said, interrupting us. "Sheriff's on the radio for you."

Nadine gave him an annoyed look but took his

walkie-talkie. "I'll be right back." She stepped down the hall, away from the noise.

Pearl's eyes lit on a memory. "He might have been wearing a hoodie."

"He?" I took her hands so she wouldn't rub holes in her skin. "What made you think it was a man?"

"I don't know. I really don't. It could have been a woman. It's just that when I think of violence, I automatically think man."

I nodded. Her ex-husband had abused her, and her perspective was filtered by her experiences. "Do you know how much higher the person's head was above the car?" That was an easier question to answer than, how tall? Height, without a measuring stick or a point of reference, was a hard thing to gauge at a distance.

She held her hands about a foot and a half. "Thereabouts," she indicated. "But the guy could have been stooped, so he could have been even taller than that. I feel about as useless as a hair on a guppy."

Pearl was on the verge of weeping, and I can't say as I blamed her, but it wouldn't help get Opal back. "Opal wouldn't want you feeling sorry for yourself," I said firmly but with as much love as I could put into the harsh words. "We need to focus all our efforts on getting her back, not on the stuff we can't do anything about. You are strong, Pearl. Much stronger than I ever thought, and you can hold it together until we get this situation settled."

"But what if she doesn't--"

"What ifs are nothing but your fear talking in your ear. You need to push it aside so we can find solutions for the real problems we're already facing, and not the ones our fears manufacture in our imagination. That's the only way we're going to help, Opal."

Pearl took a deep breath then blew it out noisily. "I know you're right, Lily. I'm just not ready to face a life without my sister in it."

I clasped her shoulder and gave it squeeze. "Then we need to make sure we find her." A good place to start was Abby's apartment. "Why did you come back here?"

"Opal insisted. She's so headstrong. She told me Abby kept a diary using a code they'd made up when Abby was a girl. They used to write letters to each other using it. Then when Abby got older, she'd confided to Opal that she still used the code to keep her private thoughts private. Opal had wanted me to find the diary."

"Did she think Abby might have written something that could point us in the right direction of who killed her?"

Pearl shrugged, her thin shoulders looking bonier and her eyes puffy as fatigue set in. "Possibly, but I think she was more worried Melinda would find it. Abby had a bit of a wild streak. There would be things in there she wouldn't want her mother to find out. Melinda had helped Abby with the code when she was young, so it wouldn't have taken much for her to figure it out."

It really had been a burn-the-porn-stash-and-wipe-the-search-history scenario. "While I respect having a friend's back, even in death, you should have told the police, or at least me. I would have made sure nothing of Abby's private thoughts were made public unless it had to do with her death."

"I know, but you know Opal. I can't talk her out of a darn thing when she gets her mind set to a course of action."

"I know. Did you manage to find the journal?"

Pearl gave me a flat stare.

"You did, didn't you?"

She lifted her blouse and pulled a leather-bound, five-by-eight notebook from the elastic waistband of her pants. She handed it over but didn't let go. "The police see *nothing* unless you find something that can point to who kidnapped Opal or Abby's killer, agreed?"

I nodded. "Agreed."

Deputy Shobe walked over to us, and I slipped the journal into my bag before he could see it. "Ms. Dixon, I'm going to take you down to the station now. We've set up a family room for you, and we'll keep you updated as we find out anything new."

"Do you want me to go with you?" I asked Pearl.

"I want you looking for my sister." She hugged me, the gesture making Shobe back a few feet away to give us space as if he were afraid she'd hug him next. In my ear, she said, "Replace every letter with the seventh letter ahead of it in the alphabet chain. A is H, Y is F, and so on."

"I understand," I said. We parted. It hurt how lost Pearl looked as Deputy Shobe escorted her from the building, and I couldn't bear the idea that she was going to have to endure the night alone. So, I called Parker.

He answered on the first ring. "What's up, buttercup?"

I fought the urge to cry. As I'd told Pearl, it wouldn't do Opal any good. "Opal Dixon is missing. She might have been taken."

"What?" I heard Smooshie barking in the background. "Sorry," he said, "I was fixing to take her outside. Hold on." I heard him say, "Calm down, girl. We'll go in a minute." He got back on the phone. "Now say that again. Opal is missing?"

"Yes. Pearl's on her way to the sheriff's station to wait. Bobby Morris has called in off-duty deputies, and they've put almost every patrol vehicle out on the streets searching for Opal."

"Where are you?"

"I'm at the Sunset Apartments. Opal was kidnapped across the street from here." I told him everything I knew up to that point, with the exception of the journal. I didn't want any of the uniforms to overhear that part.

"Do you want me to come down there? Dad and I can help with the search." That's right, Greer had spent the evening with his son.

"Does Greer know a Bob Tolliver?" I asked.

"Dad," he said off the phone. "Do you know Bob Tolliver?"

"Sure. He's a customer. I've known him for years," I heard Greer answer.

"Good," I told Parker. "Can you guys find Bob

Tolliver and see if he'll go down to the police station and stay with Pearl until this is over?"

"If it will help," Parker said.

"It will."

"Stay safe, Lily."

I melted a little. "I love you, too, Parker."

We hung up, and I went outside, crossed the parking lot and street, until I was with Reggie and the crime techs at the place where Opal's sedan had been sitting. "Find anything?"

Reggie shook her head. "Nothing that will point us in the right direction."

I gave her a gentle nudge with my shoulder. "I might have something."

"Oh yeah?"

"Get Nadine and tell her we'll be on the second floor if she needs us. Lacy's apartment is close and mostly private."

"You sure Lacy's going to be okay with us turning her place into kidnap central?"

I nodded, remembering what she'd said about Opal helping her mom. "I think she'll want to help any way she can."

It felt good to have a plan, even if I wasn't sure where it would land us. What had gotten Abby murdered? Work or personal? Was the killer also Opal's kidnapper? If so, what did the killer think Opal knew about the murder?

I hoped these and more questions would be answered when we deciphered Abby's most private musings.

CHAPTER 16

Lacy's apartment was a mirrored layout to Abby's. Living room and kitchen on one said, bathroom, utility room, and bedroom on the other. But where Abby had made a book nook, Lacy had set up a toddler bed for her son, Paulie. I was glad she was finally gaining traction again with the nursing home job and school on the horizon. This one-bedroom apartment wasn't going to be big enough once Paulie started school.

"Christ," Lacy hissed. "When you didn't show, I just thought you'd flaked on me. I can't believe Opal's been kidnapped. Do you think the police will find her?"

"Yes. Unquestionably," I said, because the alternative was too awful to entertain. "Do you mind if Reggie and I do a little brainstorming up here?"

"No," Lacy said. She ran her fingers through her hair in a self-conscious gesture, and she was in pajamas. "I changed for bed when I thought you weren't coming."

"You're fine," I told her. "I should have called you."

Nadine arrived with Reggie. The scene had been secured and other deputies were taking statements from neighbors, so she decided her time was best spent focusing on the diary with us. While we had booze, no one drank any. Instead, Lacy put on a pot of coffee, and we all caffeinated hard. I carefully tore out the most recent pages of the journal and handed them out. I didn't like damaging the book like that, but it was the fastest way to get the most information. Opal needed us to work with a sense of urgency.

"Remember," I said, trying to keep my promise to Pearl, "if it's not pertinent to Opal kidnapping or Abby's death, we didn't see it."

"Got it," Lacy said with all seriousness. "I'll never breathe a word."

"Thanks." I had been mostly talking to her, because she was the wild card in the group, so her assurance eased my worry.

"Abby mentions missing narcotics including oxycodone, fentanyl patches, and something called benzodie…benzodeeah. Crap. I can't pronounce it," Nadine said.

"Benzodiazepines," Reggie helped.

"It's a group of medications like Ativan and Xanax used for anxiety, acute depression, and sometimes seda-tion," Lacy said. "I learned about it in my CMT course. We have a supply of prefilled syringes of Lorazepam, the generic of Ativan, in the med room just in case any of the residents get violent." She frowned.

"And it's not recommended for elderly patients,"

Reggie said. "It can make them unsteady and confused. It's akin to chemically restraining them. Something I'm not crazy about. Besides, it's habit forming, and the side effects when you try to take someone off the drug is much the same as alcohol withdrawal. Not good."

"We have a lot of residents on the pill form," Lacy said. "They can get a bit loopy when they take the drug."

"Okay, so we got missing happy pills and painkillers," Nadine interjected. "Anyone else find anything?"

"What was it you were saying about the book she was reading?" Reggie asked. "She mentions a Kenneth Barlow on this page."

"That's it! That's the name of the murderer." I grabbed my phone. "I'll look him up."

"Oh," Lacy said. "Oh-oh."

"What?" the rest of us said in unison.

"This one is about having sex with her ex-husband in an on-call room at the hospital."

"How *Grey's Anatomy*," Nadine said.

Lacy blanched. "She gets pretty detailed."

"She was having sex with Dale Rogers. If they were, uhm, reconnecting again, why wouldn't Dale have just said that to Bobby this morning? Either way, I think it's safe to say that page isn't going to help us." I tore out the next entry and handed it to Lacy.

While they kept deciphering the coded entries, I typed "Kenneth Barlow killer" into my phone, just in case there were lots of Kenneth Barlows. The results that loaded made me sick to my stomach. "Insulin," I said.

"Insulin?" Reggie asked. "What about it?"

"Kenneth Barlow, a male nurse, killed his wife with insulin in 1957. It was the first reported case of insulin murder. He'd put her in the bathtub and tried to make it look like a drowning, but the pathologist noted that her eyes were dilated, which isn't consistent with drowning. There was other stuff, too, like the fact that if he'd tried to resuscitate his wife like he'd said, his clothes would have been wet and such, but there were no signs of violence on her body, and if he hadn't tried to cook up such an elaborate story, he probably wouldn't have been caught."

Reggie nodded. "Insulin metabolizes quickly, even after someone dies. Unless you can find the injection site, which is really difficult if you don't know to look for it, there is no way to tell if someone has been over-dosed with the stuff." She shook her head. "Abby's eyes were dilated, but opioids can cause the same reaction. Do you think? Could it be possible that someone injected her with a big dose of insulin?"

"Wouldn't her blood sugar have been really low?" Nadine asked.

"Not necessarily," Reggie said. "Cellular death modifies glucose levels. It might be a bit higher in a diabetic, but even a low glucose wouldn't have made me suspicious."

"Is there any way to prove she was injected?" I asked.

"If I can find the site, which is like trying to find a

needle in a haystack full of needles, there should still be some residue of the drug in the skin," she said. She stood up. "You guys keep going. I'm going to have one of the tech guys drive me to the morgue. Call me if you find something else."

Reggie grabbed her purse and left the wine chiller as she headed out.

"I think she figured out who was taking the drugs," Nadine said. "She says here, *The administrator wants me to keep my suspicions to myself about the missing schedule 2 narcotics. She says she is investigating, but I think she'd be happy to sweep it under the rug.* There is an asterisk below it with a new paragraph that says, *I plan to confront her today. I think she tampered with Mrs. Davidson in some way. There is no way her glucose sailed up to 586 from a cupcake. I found a book she was reading, and it disturbed me. I took it when she wasn't looking. I called in an anonymous tip to state. I will get to the bottom of this. I just don't understand why she'd want to hurt an elderly woman?* That's where it ends," Nadine said.

"What's the date on that one?"

"It was Friday."

"The day she died," Lacy gasped.

"Who did she say she was going to confront?" I asked.

"She doesn't give a name," Nadine replied. "It sounds like she might be talking about the administrator though."

"Ruby Davis?" Lacy asked. "Ruby is rarely on the floor, and she's intimidating. I'm not sure she could get into a med room and steal pills without someone taking notice."

"Why would someone want to tamper with Jane Davidson? If Abby was injected with a lethal dose of insulin, I wonder if the same person tried it with Jane as well?"

"That's terrible," Lacy said. "Why?"

"Maybe Jane knew something she shouldn't," Nadine said. "People have been killed for less."

"Do you know who took Mrs. Davidson out to the courtyard?" I asked Lacy.

"No one claimed responsibility."

"That doesn't surprise me. I'm pretty sure whoever wheeled her out there tried to kill her the same way they'd killed Abby." I stood up. "We're going to the hospital," I said to Nadine. "Mrs. Davidson could still be in danger. And if she's alert, maybe she can tell us who we're looking for."

Opal's life depended on it.

THE HOSPITAL VISITING HOURS WERE OVER, BUT THE STAFF didn't do much but nod when Nadine and I walked into the step-down unit, a place where they kept patients who still needed some monitoring but weren't critical. The evening nurse on duty told us Mrs. Davidson was in the third room down the hall.

"You think she'll know anything?" Nadine asked.

"I hope so." It had been almost two hours since Opal's disappearance, and my stomach burned with worry. "I really thought the police would have found her by now. How hard is it to find one car?"

"You mean a dark-blue car at night in a town with dozens of streets? And that's assuming the car hasn't been driven out of Moonrise to a more remote area."

"I get it," I said. "I know it's not your fault she's still missing. I just want to get her back before…" I couldn't finish.

"I know," Nadine said gently. "I want to find her just as much as you do. I promise."

Jane Davidson snored softly in her large hospital bed. She was hooked up to a heart monitor, and there were a few empty bags hanging from an IV pole, but nothing actually attached to her. Her television was off and the lights were dim, but it was time to wake up.

"Mrs. Davidson," I said. "It's Lily. You remember, from the manor. Opal's friend." My voice caught on Opal's name.

Mrs. Davidson didn't stir.

I rubbed my knuckle against her sternum, hoping the pain would wake her up. She moaned and blinked her eyes open. "Hello," I said. "Can you speak?"

"Wa-ter," she rasped.

"What are you doing in here?" a man asked. It was Dr. Stewart Smith, Abby's ex-lover.

"I could ask you the same thing," I said.

Nadine, dressed in civilian clothes, pulled out her badge. "Yeah, Doc. What are you doing here?"

"I'm Mrs. Davidson's doctor," he blustered. "I'm supposed to be in her room, unlike the two of you. What is this about?"

"It's about murder," I said bluntly.

His eyes widened with genuine shock. "Murder?"

Nadine crossed her arms over her chest. "Abby Rogers. And there is the attempted murder of Jane Davidson."

Mrs. Davidson, who'd been quietly watching, made at choking nose.

I frowned at Nadine.

"Sorry, Mrs. Davidson. Tact is not my strong suit."

"And neither is intelligence," Dr. Smith said. "You can't honestly believe I had anything to do with Abby killing herself or Mrs. Davidson's brittle diabetes. I'm not a magician."

His arrogance pissed me off. "No, but you are the *married* doctor who was having an affair with Abby, and she wanted to check into Mrs. Davidson's lab work, and you seemed opposed to the idea the other day at the manor."

Mrs. Davidson's eyes lit up, her shoulders bunching at what I'm sure she considered great gossip.

Dr. Smith lowered his voice. "My relationship with Abby ended two years ago. Why would I want her dead now?"

"Maybe she was threatening to tell your wife," Nadine said.

"My wife already knows," he said, clearly exasperated. "We've been in counseling for over a year. After that douche of an ex-husband tried to blackmail me, Abby gave him whatever he wanted in their divorce as long as he kept his mouth shut. I trusted Abby, but not him. Dale can be…disruptive. So, I told my wife just in case he ever spilled the beans. You see, I had absolutely no reason to kill her. I...I cared for Abby. I wouldn't have harmed her."

Nadine glanced at me. I nodded. He was telling the truth.

"Fine," she said. "But I still might have questions for you later, so keep yourself available."

"Wat...er," Mrs. Davidson rasped again.

"I'm so sorry, Mrs. Davidson." I looked around for a cup and couldn't find one.

Nadine raised her hand. "I'll find some water. You stay and keep an eye on the doctor."

"I'll be back," Dr. Smith said. "I have other patients to check on."

I snarled at him. He flushed then hurried out of the room.

After he left, I touched Mrs. Davidson's warm cheek. "Do you know who did this to you?"

Her eyelids fluttered then she nodded.

"Who? It's important."

She opened her mouth, closed it, tried to swallow, then opened it again. "Ah. Ah." She shook her head. "Waa-ter." Her voice was barely above a whisper.

"Deputy Booth is getting it for you." I looked at the door, willing Nadine to return. When she didn't, I told Mrs. Davidson, "Hang on. I'll be right back."

The corridor was dark, giving the hospital an eerie essence. I whisper-yelled, "Nadine," as I made my way down to one end before starting over to the next hall. There was a family room marked at the end of the corridor. Those places usually had coffee, water, and snacks for visitors, so I looked there next.

The door creaked as it opened, sending a shiver down my spine. The only light was the glow off a soda machine against the far wall. "Nadine?"

I sniffed the air. Coffee, cleaning chemicals, and lemons. "Nadine? Are you in here?" There was a stack of Styrofoam cups near the sink. I tried to shake the trepidation from my limbs as I got one free and turned the faucet on.

Another scent caught my attention. Sweat and body odor.

I whipped around, ready to fight. Only, I'd brought claws to a gun fight.

A hooded figure wearing a ski mask held a gun in one shaky hand and a syringe in the other, a dark blob on the floor behind her. In a menacing, low voice that I couldn't tell if it was male or female, the assailant said, "Your friend has been injected with a mild sedative but move one step closer and I'll inject her with one hundred units of insulin. It's your choice."

"Are you talking about Opal?"

"No, the deputy," the hooded figure said. It waved the gun in my direction again, and the smell of sweet citrus and sweat wafted in my direction.

I suddenly knew who was behind the mask. It made some sense now. "Does the candy help with withdrawal?" I asked. There was only one person who could have orchestrated Jane's sudden blood sugar rollercoaster, Abby's staged suicide, and Opal's kidnapping who also had the initials A.B. and had access to the medication room. "Drug addiction is an illness, Annie."

The masked assailant blinked. "How did you...?"

The clues had all been there...the lemony aroma, the shaking hands, the agitation, and the biggest one I'd missed was the initials on the murder book. A. B. for Annie Blankenship, the activity director for Moonrise Manor.

"You must have been really desperate to go after Abby," I said. "Did she know you were the one stealing narcotics? Is that why you killed her?"

Annie stopped trying to disguise her voice. "It was an accident. I didn't want to hurt Abby, but she wouldn't listen to me. I told her I was trying to quit. You're right. Addiction is an illness. I needed help, and she refused to help me." She kept the gun trained on me but fisted the syringe. "I went to her apartment to talk to her, but she was so smug. She couldn't let it go about Mrs. Davidson. I told her it was impulsive, that I hadn't really wanted to hurt Jane, but she said I had to turn myself in or she would."

"Why Mrs. Davidson?" I asked, hoping to keep her talking long enough to figure out how to get the gun and syringe away from my helpless friend.

"She saw me take some fentanyl from the narcotics cabinet. I couldn't risk her telling anyone." Annie let out a frustrated grunt. "She just smiled at me, the old cow."

The more she talked the more confidence she gained, the more she believed her own lies.

"I want to believe you, Annie. I really do, but you took the murder weapon with you to Abby's. You took the fentanyl, the oxycodone to plant, and the insulin." I pushed my power of compulsion at her and could feel her resist. Her drug use had made her immune my ability. "You wanted Abby out of the way. You wanted her dead."

Annie stepped back over Nadine.

I stepped forward, but she put the weapon to Nadine's head. "Stop right there."

I froze in place. "You can't get away with this, Annie."

"Quit saying my name!" she shrieked.

"The police have video of people going in and out of Abby's apartment for the past week. They'll find you on the night of Abby's death, and they'll find you sometime after her death when you went back to retrieve the book Abby had taken from you. They'll know it was you, and if you kill Deputy Booth," I emphasized the fact that Nadine was a police officer, "they will hang you for it." Not literally, of course, but Missouri is a death penalty state.

Annie shook her head. "I won't let them take me."

I cried out when she stuck the syringe into Nadine's arm and depressed the plunger. "I was saving that for Jane, but since you already know who I am and what I've done, my only hope is to escape. Your friend will be okay if you can get her help, so you have a choice. Follow me. Or save your friend."

She kept the gun trained on me as she inched out of the room. When the doors swung close, my knees almost buckled beneath me. I ran across the room to Nadine.

"Lily," Nadine mumbled. "Something's...wrong."

"I'm here."

"What's...wrong...with me?" Her words were slurred. "I can't...I can't..."

Insulin alone wouldn't take down a healthy adult this fast.

I saw a small glass tube on the floor next to Nadine. I pricked my finger on the end when I picked it up. A syringe, the kind that comes prefilled, but is was empty now. On the side was written, *Lorazepam 2 mg/ml*.

No wonder Nadine was out of it. Lorazepam, the stuff Lacy had talked about. She had said it was a sedative.

"Hold on," I said. "And stay awake!" I ran to the door and screamed, "Fire!" because I thought it would get more attention than "help."

I searched the wall until I found a light switch. There was a refrigerator next to the coffee machine. Inside was chocolate and vanilla pudding, along with red gelatin cups. I needed sugar, so I grabbed one of each and raced back to Nadine. "Hang in there, pal," I said, using my claw to rip the top off. "I've got you." I scooped a big finger of pudding out of the cup.

"What's...that?" Nadine asked.

"Eat up. It will make you feel better."

"Ew," she whined. Swatting at my finger. "I can't eat chocolate. Makes...me...sick."

"Since when?" I scooped up the red gelatin next. "Here."

"Mmmm. Cherry." She swallowed. I gave her some

more. A nurse finally made her way into the room. When she saw us on the floor, her mouth gaped open.

"She's been injected with one hundred units of insulin and at least two milligrams of Lorazepam," I said.

"Is she a diabetic?" the nurse asked.

"No," I told her. "She needs help. Now."

The nurse grabbed her phone from a hip holster, pushed a button, and said, "Code Blue in the step-down visitor room. Code Blue."

Within minutes, a team of nurses and an emergency-room doctor rushed in with a cartful of stuff.

Nadine's voice was already getting stronger—and I didn't mistake a single word when she said with more panic than I could bear, "I'm pregnant. The babies! Are they okay? Please tell me they're okay?"

Babies. As in more than one.

The procedure had worked. It had actually managed to produce embryos from a shifter and a human!

I wanted to be happy for Nadine and Buzz, but all I could feel was cold fear. I wanted to stick around for Nadine's sake, but she had all the help she needed to survive now, and Opal was still alone.

"You need to post someone with Jane Davidson," I told the nurse, "and call the police. The person who did this to my friend is also after Jane."

Nadine and I had disrupted the killer's plan, and Nadine had ended up the next victim.

I lit out down the hall with my phone in hand. I called Buzz. "Nadine needs you," I told him. "Get your butt over to the hospital. They're taking her to the emergency room."

"What happened?" he asked, but I didn't have time to answer.

I hung up and called Bobby Morris next. "Opal's kidnapper is Annie Blankenship. She's at the hospital," I told him. "And she," my voice caught as I said the next, "almost killed Nadine, and she still has Opal, or at least, I hope she does. I'm tracking her, but I need you to get your deputies to shut down access out of here."

"Don't go after her on your own, Lily. You're not a deputy. You're not trained for this."

I hung up on him, too. I might not be trained in police work but growing up in my community had given me all the experience I needed to make her pay.

CHAPTER 17

I ran up the hall, not caring if anyone thought I was moving too fast or too gracefully for a human. I allowed my cougar to flood my senses, and my vision, my hearing, and my sense of smell all heightened to the point of overwhelming. I stopped in Mrs. Davidson's room first. I didn't smell lemons or sweat or the killer's desperation. Was she waiting to take her shot? Or was she plotting to come back later to finish the job?

I went back out into the hall, searching for anything to point me in the right direction. I picked up traces of her here and there, a touch on a counter, a handrail, three long hallways, and finally a door marked "Stairs Level 2," where the scent trail ended. Inside the stairwell, it was two floors up to the roof and two floors down to the basement parking garage. Would she have headed up or down?

A door slam echoing from below sent me jumping over the edge to the next flight down. I would have jumped both flights, but the design of the stairwell made it impossible to see down more than one flight at a time. I landed with my knees bent to cushion the impact, then ran the rest of the way to the basement. I slammed through the door, my shoulder taking the brunt of the blow, and let out a painful roar.

Too wild. My mind raced as my animal senses, the ones that drove me to track my prey at any cost, overwhelmed my human good sense.

There was a narrow corridor with a sign pointing ahead for the garage. I recognized this place for some reason, but I couldn't put it together in my head. I just knew that my only hope to save Opal had fled in this direction.

A door rattled just ahead. My claws slid forward, my fangs elongating as I readied myself to pounce.

Reggie walked out of the room, her head down, wearing a white lab coat and carrying a clipboard.

Of course, I knew this place. This was where the hospital's morgue was located. Frustration ripped a wild noise from my throat.

Reggie snapped her gaze to me, her eyes wide with disbelief. "What's...what's wrong with you?"

I'd blown it. In my fear for Nadine and my drive to find Opal, I hadn't played it safe.

"Did you see her?" I asked. My voice sounded strange since my vocal cords were half human, half cougar now, but I forced it back to normal. My senses receded with my claws. I asked Reggie again, "Did you see her run through here?"

"Lily, I don't know what's happening," she approached me slowly. "But let me help you."

"I can't do this right now. I need to find her."

"Who?"

A car door slammed out in the garage. I heard an engine start. I wanted to explain everything to Reggie, but it would take too long.

I took off, again not bothering to modify my speed. I heard Reggie in the distance, shouting for me to wait.

I didn't. Opal couldn't wait.

The parking lot was mostly empty this time of night, so I easily spotted the red coupe backing up out of a space near the far end. And when it was facing my direction, I could see the face of the murderer as she gawked at me with disbelief.

Annie's gaze grew hard and determined right before the car accelerated toward me.

"Look out!" Reggie shouted, but I was already moving, running toward the vehicle in a game of chicken that I might not survive.

I could see Annie's eyes widening with surprise then fear as I closed the distance between us. It was only seconds, but it was as if every moment was playing out in slow motion.

I wasn't fool enough to think that I would win in a head-on collision with a twenty-five-hundred-pound hunk of metal speeding in my direction. There was a concrete support pillar to the left of me at the halfway mark, and it gave me an idea. I angled to that side of the aisle, forcing Annie to veer to her right if she wanted to mow me down.

Her eyes darted maniacally as she leaned forward in her seat when the car was only feet from me. I reached the column before her, and when the car was inches away, I launched myself into the air.

She swerved, her face aghast for the split second before I rolled over the roof of the car, tumbling to the asphalt on the other side, and she smashed into the unforgiving concrete.

I'd hit my head and blood dripped down into my eyes as I tried to get up. My ears felt stuffy, but I could hear a horn blaring like an alarm.

Then Reggie was there. "Don't try to move," she said. "Keep still. I think your arm is broken." She had her lab coat off and was pressing it to my head."

"Annie," I said.

"She's alive," Reggie said. "But unconscious."

"Opal?"

"I didn't see her in the car."

Sirens wailed. Red and blue lights swirled around the garage walls and ceilings. My hearing returned and the full blast of all the noise hit me. I winced.

"The police are here," Reggie said. "Whatever's going on with you, you need to fix it before they see you."

I blinked at her, a slow dawning of comprehension. My arms were covered in a fine layer of dark-golden fur, my nails were thick, hard, and sharp. I had changed into my half-form when Annie had charged me. No wonder she'd looked frantic and scared.

The pain was duller when I was shifted, and I knew when I pulled my cougar back, the pain would be extreme. But I'd survived extreme before, I'd survive this.

I wasn't wrong about the pain. I whimpered as I shoved my cougar back inside. The sirens had stopped. I heard Bobby Morris hollering at his deputies for someone to shut off the car alarm. Paramedics were on the scene, and I forced a smile when a familiar face knelt down next to Reggie and me. It was Robyn Patterson.

"We have to stop meeting like this, Lily," she said.

"Every friendship needs a thing," I told her. "This is ours."

She handed Reggie a wad of four by fours. "Here, Doc. This might work better."

Reggie took the lab coat off my head wound and pressed the area with the gauze pads.

"Her arm is broke," Reggie said. "We need to get it stabilized."

I knew I was still in shock, because everything happening felt almost dreamlike. My head was in Reggie's lap. I knew that now. I'd been partially shifted when she'd ran to me. I must have looked like a monster to my friend, and yet, she had stayed. She hadn't left my side.

I met her gaze. She didn't smile, but she didn't look away. Her expression told me we would have a long talk later, but right now, my health was her only concern.

"You're going to be okay," she said. "I've got you."

I believed her.

"Is she conscious, yet?" I heard Bobby say.

"Did they find Opal?" I asked Robyn.

"Not yet, but I heard they found her car abandoned out by the old Safeway."

Dread tightened in my chest. "If Annie's awake, I want to talk to her. I can make her tell us where Opal is."

"You aren't doing anything," Robyn said. "Stubborn mule." Her brown eyes were warm and pitying. I must have looked pretty bad.

It was difficult with all the commotion around me, but I swore I heard a slight *thump*. Then again. *Thump thump*. It was faint, almost like a heartbeat, but not steady or regular enough.

Thump. Thump thump.

"I hear something," I said to Reggie.

"There's a lot going on," she said.

"It's not that." I rolled off her lap, crying out as I yanked my arm free from Robyn's ministrations.

"What are you doing?" Robyn asked, grabbing me by the shoulder as I stood up. "You're going to do your-self a world of harm."

I shrugged her off and stared at Reggie. "I hear something." I put as much meaning into the words as I could to make her understand.

She nodded.

"I need everyone to be quiet," I said.

But none of the deputies would stop their incessant talking.

Thump.

"Quiet," I said again.

A high-pitched whistle shrilled, echoing off the concrete walls. Everyone stopped moving then. We all looked a Reggie, who removed a coach's whistle from between her lips. "Lily hears something, so, everyone settle down," she commanded.

Thump thump.

It was coming from the crashed vehicle, but Reggie had said Opal wasn't in the car. Then I noticed the taillight was missing on the left side. "The trunk," I said, suddenly dizzy. "Check the trunk."

Deputy Shobe reached inside the driver door. "The button isn't working," he said.

"Get something to pry this open," Bobby ordered. He was standing at the back end now. It took all my willpower not to walk over and rip the trunk open like a pop-top can. I'd already risked so much.

Bobby knew what he was doing, because within seconds of being handed a crowbar, he'd broken the latch and opened the trunk.

Inside, Opal Dixon was bound and gagged. She lay with her back to us.

"She's here!" Bobby shouted. "She's alive."

I stumbled back, as the adrenaline that had fueled me before gave way to relief.

"Medic," Reggie yelled as she lowered me to the ground. "Someone get me a damn gurney over here so we can get this woman treated." To me, she said, "Relax now, Lily. Opal is safe. You did it. You saved her. Now let me take care of you."

"Parker," I said. My voice sounded weak, and I struggled to get enough air to speak. "I want Parker." And Smooshie. I'm not sure I ever needed either of them so much.

"I'll make sure he's the first one called."

"Thank you." I gripped her wrist. "I mean it."

"I know. Now stop talking. I think you might have a punctured lung.

That would explain the sharp pain when I inhaled. "Reggie."

"Hush now."

"If I don't make it."

"You're not dying, Lily Mason."

"I know," I said, "but if I don't make it...there's a box in my hall closet under the guest towels." I smiled wanly. "Burn on death."

She snorted a laugh, tears brimming her eyes. "That's what friends are for."

CHAPTER 18

A week had passed since the night in the hospital garage, and I was finally getting out of the hospital. A broken rib had, in fact, punctured my lung, and my right ulnar bone had been snapped just above my wrist. Because of my circumstances, Reggie had performed both surgeries. I'd needed a doctor who wouldn't get too excited when I healed several times faster than the average patient.

So, I had a cast over my hand and wrist up to my mid-forearm, but at this point, I wasn't having any swelling or pain. Reggie had taken an x-ray and said the bone looked as if it had been in a cast for several weeks.

Opal had been banged up and bruised, but other than that, she'd been able to go home and be with Pearl.

I'd gotten a good giggle when they'd come to visit me a few days ago.

Apparently, Bob Tolliver hadn't left Pearl's side

since the night of Opal's kidnapping, and Opal blamed me for the "Canker sore on her ass," as she'd called Bob, "that wouldn't leave." Although she'd confided in me that she was glad Pearl had the distraction. Pearl had spent her entire adult life as the sister who had needed rescuing, and now that the shoe was on the other foot, Pearl had become entirely too fussy and bossy. "She makes me get up and stand every waking hour, she won't let me lift anything, and she keeps forcing protein and vitamin C down my throat because Reggie Crawford told her it was good for wound healing."

In other words, Pearl was doing everything possible to take the best care of her sister and get her back to fighting form.

Nadine had been put on bedrest at home for a couple of days, so I hadn't seen her since that night. Buzz said she was doing well, but I didn't think I'd rest easy until I saw for myself. Reggie visited me every day, and she never asked me about my hairy condition. She just accepted that I would tell her about it when I was ready.

I'd had several discussions with Parker and Buzz, and we decided as a family that Reggie and Greer should be in the know. "But no one else," Buzz insisted. "I don't want to have to move Nadine away from the town she loves because everyone knows our secret."

I'd agreed with him.

Also, Reggie had said that Greer never got around to telling Parker about the engagement because of Opal's kidnapping.

As to Annie Blankenship, she was in jail. She'd confessed to everything, though she still didn't believe it was her fault. Abby had found out about her stealing and abusing narcotics. Annie said she hadn't planned to kill Abby, she'd only gone over to the apartment to beg her not to tell. She'd even joined a twelve-step program to quit. But, she'd complained, Abby wouldn't hear her out and was determined to turn her in. Mostly because of Annie trying to send Jane Davidson into a hyper-glycemic coma.

So, Annie, who was bigger than Abby, held her down and slapped a high-dose fentanyl patch on her until she was compliant, put her to bed, then injected her with a hundred units of fast-acting insulin.

It's hard to claim there was no premeditation when you bring the murder weapons with you. And that's exactly what the prosecuting attorney said when he levied the charge of murder in the first degree against her.

Poor Jane Davidson. She'd been in the hallway when Annie stole some drugs. She'd just injected herself with half a syringe of Lorazepam, and in her drug-addled stupor, she'd been certain that Mrs. Davidson had seen her.

Jane Davidson hadn't seen a thing! And Annie's first attempt on the elderly lady's life had been what had made Abby suspicious. If Annie hadn't been paranoid enough to do something so impulsive, Abby might not have ever found out.

And dear Abby, she'd been on the verge of getting her life back. Most of her journal entries had been filled with hope for a new life with her ex-husband. She had still loved him, and the fact that he was getting help for his anger issues had made her want to give him a second chance.

I was glad Annie would spend the rest of her life in a cell. She'd taken the life of a young woman who had a lot to live for, and if she'd had her way, she would have had four more victims, Jane, Opal, Nadine, and myself.

As it was, I was ready to move on. I'd missed the first week and a half of classes. Dr. Cramer said he wouldn't dock my grade, seeing as how I had an excuse from a doctor and the sheriff, and my other professors had said as long as I could get caught up, they wouldn't count the absences against me, either.

Nadine, Buzz, Reggie, Greer, and Parker were planning a homecoming party for me tonight. The hospital had made me stir crazy, so I was giddy with excitement that I was finally getting out. Even so, with all our secrets, I had a feeling the evening was going to be an interesting night of reveals.

Parker picked me up from the hospital with Smooshie and Elvis in the back of his truck. I cried out in surprise when Smooshie scrabbled over the middle console to occupy the space of my lap.

"Smooshie!" Parker said. "No."

"I'm fine," I said, wrapping my arms around her warm body. "I'm better than fine." Goddess, I'd missed her more than I had thought possible. Parker had brought me videos and pictures, but nothing was as good as the real thing. "You smell like corn chips," I told her. "It's making me hungry."

Parker laughed. "You're always hungry."

"That's the truth."

I'd snuggled into Smooshie, her presence making me more calm than I had been all week, so I didn't notice until we were driving out of town that we were driving out of town. "I thought we were all meeting at your house."

"We are," he said. "My house is on 1031 Northwest 400 Road."

That was my address.

I stared at Parker, who had a satisfied expression on his face and amended my thinking. "That's our address," I said out loud.

He chuckled. "It sure is."

"What are you planning?"

"You'll see." And that's all he'd tell me on the subject for the ten minutes it took to pull into the driveway.

Buzz's car and Greer's truck were parked out front. The lights were all on in the house. Not the trailer. The house.

"Buzz and my dad are cooking," Parker said.

"That's great. Are we eating on the floor?" I asked. I opened the door and slid out, Smooshie jumping just past me. Elvis got out on Parker's side.

"We made arrangements," Parker said as we walked up the steps. "Close your eyes."

"You want me to break another arm?"

He positioned himself behind me on the front stoop and put his hand over my eyes. "Be a sport."

"I always am."

I let him guide me inside, a flutter of excitement fueled my anticipation. Parker dropped his hand.

We were standing in the foyer, where I could see both the kitchen and living room. A beautiful hand-sanded golden oak table with six twisted oak chairs sat in the center of my large kitchen. The living room had a brown pit set with a square golden oak coffee table with storage, and two matching end tables. A television stand was set up across from it, and there was a large TV sitting on top.

Everything had been stuff that I'd wanted. Like the sofa. I'd mentioned to Reggie a few months back, when she'd taken me shopping to get herself a new lamp, that I'd want something like that when my house was ready. I gave her a sideways glance, and she grinned. The kitchen table had been when Greer had talked me into going antiquing with him.

Everything they'd put in the house, down to the throw rug in the living room, had been something I'd said I'd wanted or needed. I was at a loss for words.

"Oh, Lily," Nadine said. "Don't cry. If you cry, I'll cry."

"Me too," Reggie agreed.

"You guys love me," I said. "You really love me."

"Rein it in, Sally Fields," Greer said. "Before this party turns into a therapy session."

"How did you guys do all this?" I asked. "It's everything!"

"We've been buying stuff and putting it in storage for months, just waiting for your house to be ready," Parker said.

"Our house."

He grinned. "Ours."

Reggie and Nadine shuffled me into the living room. The guys brought in drinks for us.

Greer stood behind the couch where Reggie sat and put his hand on her shoulder. "I'd like everyone to sit down for a minute," he said. "I have something I'd like to say."

Oh my gosh, my heart picked up a beat. Let the reveals begin!

Parker sat next to me. I took his hand and held my breath.

Greer cleared his throat. "I....we, Reg and I, we want to share with you." He rubbed his free hand through his hair, a nervous gesture I'd seen more than once from Parker. "Ah, hell. I've asked Reg to marry me, and she said yes."

Parker's fingers squeezed mine. The breath whooshed out of me. Nadine and Buzz were already offering congratulations, and I was grinning wide, but Parker had remained quiet.

I looked at him. "Are you okay?"

Parker nodded then got up and went to his father. He smiled. "Congratulations, Dad. I'm happy for you." They hugged, and I cried.

I joined Nadine with Reggie as she put on the ring, finally able to wear it. We oohed and ahhed for a few minutes. Before Nadine said, "Since we're telling each other stuff. Buzz and I have some news of our own."

"Are you two engaged, also?" Reggie asked excitedly.

"No," Nadine said. "Better. We're pregnant!"

There was a chorus of cheers all around.

"That's amazing," I said. "Are the babies okay after last week?"

"Babies?" Reggie said. "As in more than one?"

Nadine laughed. "As in three," she said. "Our California trip wasn't a vacation. We went to see a fertility specialist. He was able to implant five fertilized eggs. We lost two of them, but three have taken. And I'm past the first month, so it's a good sign."

"It sure is," Reggie said. She hugged Nadine tight. "Whatever you need, I am here for these little ones."

"Same," I said. "I can't wait to meet my little cousins."

"You mean nieces or nephews, Auntie Lily," Nadine said. "You and Reggie aren't just my best friends. You're my family. My kids are going to love you the way I do."

The men were all handshakes and bro hugs in the background. There had been so much good news tonight, it seemed like as good a time as ever to come clean with Reggie and Greer.

"Uhm," I said when there was a momentary lull in the conversation. "Buzz and I would like to share something with you all as well."

Nadine and Parker knew what was coming next, and they nervously took their positions beside us.

"Greer. Reggie. You guys might want to sit down for this." I didn't know what I was going to do if Greer freaked out.

Reggie took Greer's hand. "Come on," she said. They sat down. "Go on, Lily. We're ready."

I wasn't sure the best way to approach this, but Nadine has suggested we start with a fictional introduction, so I said, "Have you ever seen any shows about werewolves, vampires, witches, that kind of thing?"

"Reggie made me watch that *Underworld* movie. She loves all that paranormal mumbo-jumbo," Greer said. "Is that the kind of thing you mean?"

"Yes, that's, well… That's sort of the idea."

Greer's eyes widened. "Did you guys write a book? A movie script? Are you getting a movie made?"

"Let her talk," Reggie said.

"We didn't write a book or movie," I told him. "But those ideas, they come from somewhere. You know, a type of reality that exists, but not usually in the way it's portrayed." Though, like in *Underworld*, there were a lot of politics in the shifter and witch world. "What I mean is, the myths are often based on real life."

"Are you a vampire, Lily?" Greer asked. "Because, I've seen you in the sun. You didn't go up in flames."

He joked because he was uncomfortable. I'd seen Greer do it in other situations where he felt confused or conflicted.

"No worries." I smiled. "I'm not a vampire. However, Buzz and I are different from other people."

"Different how?"

Wow, this was a much harder conversation than I had imagined. I mean, I couldn't just blurt it out, "hey, I turn into a cougar sometimes," and shifting without an explanation would probably give him a heart attack.

"Oh, for heaven's sake," Buzz said. "We're therianthropes, Greer. Reggie. Shifters is a more common term. We're part human, part animal. Cougar, to be exact. It doesn't change who we are fundamentally. It just means that every once in a while, we're furry and run around on four paws."

Greer's brows dipped. His frown deepened. Then he laughed. "You almost had me going there for a minute! Fur and four paws."

"Greer," Reggie said. "I think you need to listen to them."

Buzz sighed. "Seeing is believing."

"Don't be scared, Dad. It's really pretty neat, once you're used to the idea."

"Scared?" Greer stared at his son. "Of what?"

Buzz took his shirt off as his body began to shift and morph, hair sprouting across his skin as his human self became beast.

In seconds, a large tawny cougar with a copper-dark muzzle stepped out of Buzz's jeans, its long tail curling around Nadine's leg.

Greer and Reggie both gasped, but they didn't run away screaming. I took that as a good sign.

"I knew it," Reggie finally said. "I just knew it!"

"How?" I asked.

"That night you flew ten feet through the air to tackle Rachel outside the bar. Your eyes were glowing green, and even with a major rush of adrenaline, I didn't think any regular human could leap that high or that far and land with the grace you exhibited. Then last week with that car, and the fur, of course, and claws, and let's not forget the fangs," she said quickly in one rambling breath. "I guess it just confirmed what I had already suspected."

"There's a mountain lion in the living room," Greer said dully.

"Uh oh," Nadine said. "I think he's in shock."

Buzz picked up his jeans with his teeth and loped off to a more private location. He came back a few minutes later.

"Well, do you have any questions?"

"How many people know about this?" Greer asked.

"In Moonrise, only the people in this room," Buzz said. "And that's the way we'd like to keep it."

Greer nodded. "And Lily? You can do this too?"

"Yes."

"All the time," Parker said. "She likes to take Smooshie on runs through the woods."

His dad's eyes bulged.

"Please, don't help, babe," I said.

"And what about Nadine. Are your babies going to be, you know, shifters?" Greer asked.

"No," Buzz said. "The doctor we saw has perfected a technique so that shifters and humans can mate, but the offspring are always human."

Greer nodded in my direction. "And you, Lily? Are you and Parker going to have children?"

I didn't want to have to explain that I had a witch grandparent that made me different from Buzz. Parker and I were fated. We had each other's scents. He could get me pregnant. But the truth was, neither of us wanted children. We had a whole rescue of furry babies that needed our love and attention.

"We won't be," I said.

"We're happy, Dad. I love my life with Lily. She's the only one for me. And we both love you. All of you, so we wanted to be honest about our lives. I hope you can be happy for us."

Greer got up again. "The roast is done. Why don't we go eat and we can talk more? I don't really understand all this, but I'm open to hearing you. Besides, everything sounds a little less crazy on a full stomach."

As if cued, my belly growled. I didn't know what would happen next, but my circle of family in Moonrise was getting bigger and stronger.

Parker put his arms around me. "You okay?"

"Uh hmm," I said, leaning my head back against his chest. Smooshie trotted in an rammed her head between my knees.

"She missed you," he said.

"I missed her, too."

"How do you like the house?"

"It's more than I ever expected. It means so much, Parker."

He pressed his lips to my ear. "Wait until you see the bedroom."

I curled my palm against his cheek and looked around. Our family was talking and laughing in the kitchen. Elvis had flopped on a large dog bed at the end of the foyer, and Smooshie was beating me with her tail. All was right.

"I can't believe it," I told Parker.

"What?"

"I can't believe I'm finally home. I made it."
Parker wrapped me tighter and kissed my cheek.
"Welcome home, Lily."

The End

PARANORMAL MYSTERIES & ROMANCES

BY RENEE GEORGE

Witchin' Impossible Cozy Mysteries
www.witchinimpossible.com
Witchin' Impossible (Book 1)
Rogue Coven (Book 2)
Familiar Protocol (Booke 3)
Mr & Mrs. Shift (Book 4)

Barkside of the Moon Mysteries
www.barksideofthemoonmysteries.com
Pit Perfect Murder (Book 1)
Murder & The Money Pit (Book 2)
The Pit List Murders (Book 3)
Pit & Miss Murder (Book 4)
The Prune Pit Murder (Book 5)

Peculiar Mysteries
www.peculiarmysteries.com
You've Got Tail (Book 1) FREE Download
My Furry Valentine (Book 2)

Thank You For Not Shifting (Book 3)
My Hairy Halloween (Book 4)
In the Midnight Howl (Book 5)
My Peculiar Road Trip (Magic & Mayhem) (Book 6)
Furred Lines (Book7)
My Wolfy Wedding (Book 8)
Who Let The Wolves Out? (Book 9)
My Thanksgiving Faux Paw (Book 10)

Madder Than Hell
www.madder-than-hell.com
Gone With The Minion (Book 1)
Devil On A Hot Tin Roof (Book 2)
A Street Car Named Demonic (Book 3)

Hex Drive
https://www.renee-george.com/hex-drive-series
Hex Me, Baby, One More Time (Book 1)
Oops, I Hexed It Again (Book 2)
I Want Your Hex (Book 3)

ABOUT THE AUTHOR

I am a USA Today Bestselling author who writes paranormal mysteries and romances because I love all things whodunit, Otherworldly, and weird. Also, I wish my pittie, the adorable Kona Princess Warrior, and my beagle, Josie the Incontinent Princess, could talk. Or at least be more like Scooby-Doo and help me unmask villains at the haunted house up the street.

When I'm not writing about mystery-solving werecougars or the adventures of a hapless psychic living among shapeshifters, I am preyed upon by stray kittens who end up living in my house because I can't say no to those sweet, furry faces. (Someone stop telling them where I live!)

I live in Mid-Missouri with my family and I spend my non-writing time doing really cool stuff...like watching TV and cleaning up dog poop.

Follow Me On Bookbub!

Printed in Great Britain
by Amazon

21619038R00123